CW00862917

Frank Morgan

STORY

FANTAIL PUBLISHING

AN IMPRINT OF PUFFIN ENTERPRISES

Published by the Penguin Group
27 Wrights Lane, London W8 5TZ

First published by Fantail Publishing, 1989

Copyright © Licensing Management International, 1989

All rights reserved

014 0901280

10 9 8 7 6 5 4 3 2 1

Made and printed in Great Britain by
Richard Clay Ltd, Bungay, Suffolk

All rights reserved. Without limiting the
rights under copyright reserved above, no
part of this publication may be reproduced,
stored in or introduced into a retrieval
system, or transmitted, in any form or by
any means (electronic, mechanical, or
photocopying, recording or otherwise),
without the prior written permission of
both the copyright owner and the above
publisher of this book.

THE
Frank Morgan
STORY

Elizabeth Coleman

FANTAIL

THE
Frank Morgan
STORY

Elizabeth Coleman

FANTAIL

chapter one

Frank Morgan woke to the sound of the surf pounding into shore at pretty Summer Bay beach. There was nothing like the ocean, he'd always thought, to wash the troubles of the day away before the day began.

That was why he loved the little flat behind the Summer Bay store, even though his spinster landlady, Celia Stewart, got a bit hard to handle at times. Celia was constantly fishing for gossip and lecturing Frank about 'moral fibre'. But still, it was worth putting up with – worth it for the quick step across to the sea – and worth it especially for this part of the day – waking up to the windswept waves.

Frank put his hands beneath his head and gazed up at the ceiling. A huge smile of joy spread its way across his face. Today was the last day he'd listen to the sea alone. Tomorrow morning, and the morning after that, and the morning after that, and every morning, forever – Bobby would wake up beside him.

Beautiful Bobby, his future wife. In fact – he glanced over at his bedside clock – she'd be Mrs Morgan in just under six hours! He loved the sound of it – Bobby Morgan. He closed his eyes and conjured up a picture of his bride. Spirited, rebellious Bobby Simpson, whose loyalty matched her fierce independence. She'd always known they were meant for each other. She'd waited for him without question while he chased something that soon ceased to matter. Then one day he'd opened his eyes and realized all he wanted to see was a little girl with a fiery temper whose honesty had touched his heart. Turning on his side, Frank shivered as he thought how close he'd come to missing out on this day of days – and all because of conniving Roo Stewart.

His mind went back to a year ago. Was it only that recently? It seemed a lifetime. He'd thought he was getting married then – but he'd thought a lot of things in those days, and believed a lot of phoney stories spun to him by Roo.

Roo was beautiful, sure, there was no denying that – and she'd done a lot of growing up lately; but the Roo Stewart of a year ago had set out to coldly trap Frank. And, worst of all, she'd almost succeeded! He shuddered at the memory.

Roo had tricked him into sleeping with her,

knowing they'd be caught in the act by her furious father Alf. Then she'd announced they'd agreed to get married. Frank hadn't minded – he loved her deeply. Well, he'd thought he loved her anyway. He knew now that it was nothing – just a simple passing infatuation, compared to the depth of his feelings for Bobby. He smiled again at the thought of his bride. He should send Roo a thank you card! If she hadn't broken down at the altar and confessed that he wasn't her baby's father, he wouldn't be lying here now, five and a half hours away from marrying Bobby Simpson.

He pictured her standing beside him in her wedding dress, and his heart filled with so much pride he thought that it might burst. This afternoon Frank Morgan and Bobby Simpson would become man and wife, and nothing could possibly spoil their wedding.

But even as he told himself so, Frank knew that wasn't completely true, for neither bride nor groom would have their parents present. In fact, poor Bobby didn't even know who her parents were. She'd told Frank she'd given up her quest to find them, but he knew that secretly she would have loved to invite them – whoever they were – to witness her wedding vows.

And as for him, well, there was no point in

denying it, he'd wanted his parents present too. Miss Molloy from the Department of Youth and Community Services had tried to track them down for him, but they'd both done a 'disappearing act' over the last few years. It seemed they didn't care enough about Frank to keep in contact with the Department that had fostered him out to the Fletchers. Frank had to admit it hurt him deeply, but he knew his sadness would be solved in the long-run. He and Bobby would have a family of their own, and they'd work their guts out to give their kids a wonderfully happy life – the kind of life they'd never known in their own troubled childhoods.

Childhood? Huh! What childhood? Frank tossed in his bed. Before he'd reached the haven of life with Tom and Pippa, Frank's early years had been characterized by petty crimes and parental neglect. An attempted bank robber, at the age of eight! What kind of life was that for any little boy?

He closed his eyes and it all came flooding back, as though it were only yesterday. The sounds, the hungry smell of the streets, the oppressive air of the inner-city . . . He was eight again, with his gang of friends . . .

Smash!!! The rock ripped right through the classroom window, shattering it in a million pieces, and landed with a thud on the timber floor. A robust little boy with red hair and freckles, turned excitedly to his dark-haired mate.

'See that Morgan? What a smasheroo!'

'Let's get outa here!' screamed another of the four boys. 'Someone'll call the cops!'

They scrambled away as though chased by a demon – out of the playground, into the street, past Old Papadopolous' fruit shop, through the milk bar, and 'round the corner to their secret hideout in the little lane behind Wilson Street. They stopped in a panting huddle, beaming at their latest exploit.

The boy who'd thrown the stone looked eagerly at the dark-haired lad, leader of the gang.

'D'ya see it, did ya? Made a loud smash eh, Morgan?'

Eight-year-old Frank Morgan shrugged his shoulders, unimpressed.

'Yeah, it was all right, I s'pose. Got nothin' on what my dad did once, but.'

'Yeah? What'd he do?!'

Frank's dad was a real live criminal! The little boys never tired of hearing about his exploits.

They gathered around to listen again, a motley little bunch in ragged shorts and old T-shirts.

The red-haired and freckled boy, Mickey Jones, was Frank's best friend. He was sixth in a family of eight kids who lived down the street from the Morgans. The Jones' didn't have much money, and what little they did have, Mickey's dad spent on booze. If Mickey didn't come home for dinner it meant one less mouth to feed, and that was a relief to Mrs Jones, who never said much; just clasped her rosary beads and prayed that things would one day get better.

'Grub's' real name was Peter – Peter Dannuci. He was bigger than all the others. Mr Papadopolous in the fruit shop thought that Grub was twelve! He had a big brother called Gino, with an awesome reputation for bashing up anyone who tried to stand in his way. The grown-ups all said Grub was heading in the same direction – but Peter's dad didn't mind. He said it was best to be able to stick up for yourself from an early age. No good being a wimp, Mr Dannuci declared. It didn't get you anywhere. Besides, if Peter could look after himself, it meant that Mr Dannuci could visit gambling places without having to worry about Grub. Grub's mum had left a few years ago.

Sam Green was quiet – so quiet some of the older kids said he was a moron. But Frank,

Mickey and Grub knew different. Sam mightn't say much, be he laughed lots, and he was always willing to help them out with any scheme they had going. Slight, fair-haired Sam lived with his grandma a few streets away from Frank and Mickey. No one really knew where his parents were, 'til one day he'd told Frank that they'd dumped him on his grandma three years ago. A lot of the kids thought Sam's grandma was a mean old woman, but Sam said she wasn't so bad. She made him sausages and mashed potato, and she fixed his pants when they had holes.

The three boys gathered around Frankie, their leader, eager to hear the latest installment about Frank's 'crim' father, Les.

'Dad broke ten windows in a jewellery shop once,' boasted Frank. 'He went through 'em, one by one, smashin' 'em to bits with his rifle – Smash! Smash! Smash!'

'All these sirens started going, and the cops were on their way, but Dad was too quick for 'em. He made all the people in the shop lie down on the floor – told 'em he'd shoot 'em sky-high if they moved! And he went through all the windows and took all the jewels and the necklaces and the rings, and then twenty cops came, and he made them give him their guns, and then they had to lie down on the floor too, and he took all the jewels and put them in his bag, and then he fired three shots in the air just to scare 'em – Pow! Pow! Pow! – and then he escaped, and he came home, and he gave all the jewels to Mum.'

The last part wasn't true – Les Morgan had arranged for a 'fence', a criminal colleague, to sell the jewellery for him. But Frank had always secretly wished his father had stolen it for his mother, Helena. And so Frank pretended that's what had happened. And he found that after pretending for a while, he started to believe his own fib. So it was almost like his dad had given his mum the jewels anyway.

Les Morgan was a rough and ready petty criminal whose crimes had grown in gravity with the years. Frank was just two years old the first time his father was arrested, for housebreaking. Les spent two years in gaol, was released for six months, and was then sent back 'inside' for assault occasioning grievous bodily harm. Frank was five and a half when Les was next released. He spent the following two years avoiding arrest, until being imprisoned for drug pushing. It was during these two turbulent years that Frank grew to worship his wayward father. In spite of suffering frequent beatings, he built Les Morgan up in his mind to be a modern-day Robin Hood. Frank's dad always saved the day. He was the greatest criminal of all time, ever!

In fact, although Frank didn't know it, Les' account of his jewellery heist bore little resemblance to the truth. Les was fond of fibs himself, and spent a large part of his life telling lies. But little Frank, in his blind hero-worship, wasn't aware of that. And neither were his three best buddies, who secretly wished they had a father just like Frank's.

'What happened then?!' asked Mickey.

'Nothing. No one guessed it was him. He just strolled down the pub and sank a few beers with his mates, like it was any other day.' Frank repeated the story word-for-word, exactly as Les had told it.

'He shoulda shot someone,' said Grub.

'Should not!' yelled Frank. He hated anyone criticising his father – not that they dared to very often. What would Grub know? He was just a kid!

'He didn't have to shoot anyone. They were all so scared of him they did exactly what he said anyway. The cops were shaking like leaves!'

'All twenty of 'em?' asked Mickey.

'All twenty of 'em,' boasted Frank.

Grub stood up and raised a pretend rifle to his shoulder. He squinted his eye in concentration.

9

'Everybody lie down on the floor or I blow your brains out!'

He pointed the rifle in Sam's direction.

'That means you, Dummy! Now!'

Sam smiled and lay down on the ground, pretending to be scared of Grub and his imaginary gun.

'Stop bein' stupid Grub,' ordered Frank. 'Get up, Greeno.'

Even though Grub was much bigger than Frank, he obeyed him instantly, as always. The fellas all knew you didn't muck around with someone who had a dad like Les Morgan.

'Just foolin' around,' he muttered.

'Yeah – foolin' around, all right.' jeered Frank. 'You don't know nothin' about what it's really like to pull a proper job. You know what my dad would do if he saw you pretendin' like that? He'd laugh! He'd laugh his head off, 'cause he knows what it's like to be the real thing.'

The gang fell silent. They couldn't argue with that. Les Morgan's reputation was legendary.

'Ya gonna see him soon, Frankie?'

Sam Green dared to ask the question the other boys were too scared to pose. They all knew Frank hadn't seen his dad since he'd gone back to prison six months ago. His mother, Helena, refused to let him visit Les in gaol. She said it wasn't the place for kids. Frank didn't care about that. All he wanted was to see his father and tell him all about his plans to follow in Les' heroic footsteps. The fellas had all seen Frank crying in frustration when his mother refused to allow him to go, and they'd all suffered the brunt of his black moods as a result.

'Yeah. Next week,' Frank answered defiantly.

'Did your Mum say you can go?' asked Mickey.

'Nuh. But she will,' said Frank. 'If she doesn't let me I'll break in anyway. They can break outa gaols, so I can break inta one. Be easy.'

'Can I come with ya?' asked Grub.

'Yeah – me too!' cried Mickey.

'Get lost!' Frank yelled. 'No way! Me and Dad have gotta talk about stuff youse wouldn't under-stand.'

The other boys were instantly curious.

'Like what?'

'Yeah – like what?'

'Are you plannin' a job together, Frankie?' asked Grub in awe.

'Yeah. A real big one!'

Mickey's eyes opened wide with excitement.

'You gonna rob another jewellery store?!'

'You gonna steal a car?!'

Frank felt his chest swell with pride at Mickey and Grub's envious faces.

'Maybe. Dad said I can't tell. No one. Especially youse.'

Then he caught Sam's eye. Sam wasn't saying anything. It made Frank feel uncomfortable. He had the feeling Sam knew he was lying. He jumped to his feet.

'I'm goin'.'

The other boys stood up to follow him.

'I said I'm goin'! By meself.'

'Where to?' asked Mickey.

'Home. What's it to ya?'

'You goin' to the gaol this arvo?' asked Grub.

'Maybe,' Frank answered defensively.

'Wanna nick some chocolates from the milk bar on the way home?' asked Mickey.

'Nuh. That's for kids. See yas later.'

'Yeah. See ya.'

Frank turned around and walked away, carefully avoiding Sam's big sad eyes.

As he trudged down the narrow lane on his way home to their run-down terrace, he made a decision. He would force his mum to let him see his dad if it was the last thing he ever did! He wished he'd thought to pinch a bottle of booze from the rack out the front of the liquor store. If he gave his mother some whisky or something, she'd let him go to the gaol for sure. He kicked a stone along the cracked concrete. His mum seemed to like liquor better than anything else these days. Better than him, for sure. He wished she was still like she used to be . . .

Frank remembered times when she'd laughed and sung, and told him magical stories about elves and fairies, princes and kings, and little black ducklings that cried. She was so pretty in those days, his mum. Her hair was long, dark and wavy, and she had big brown eyes that smiled down at him and made him feel everything was all right. She hugged him every day and called him her 'agapimu'. But that was before Les got out of gaol.

When Frank's Dad came back to live with them, things started changing. Helena didn't talk to Frank much any more. She hardly even looked at him. She wandered around seeming sad about something, and she jumped like a frightened rabbit when Les called her name. Sometimes Frank heard his dad yelling at her late at night. She'd cry and say 'Please don't hurt me!', then Les would storm off to the pub, and she'd lock herself in their room.

Once Helena's mother came around while Les was out doing a job. She was saying all kinds of horrible things about Les that made Frank mad. 'That tembelis is ruining you!' she cried. 'He has wrecked your life! And the child will be no better! There is badness in him. I can see it already!' Then she shook her head at Helena and sighed 'And you – you with your drinking. You think it isn't obvious? You think your mama and papa don't notice these things? Well I am fed-up to here, Helena. I wash my hands of you! Your papa and me don't want to know nothing about you no more!'

She didn't see seven and a half year old Frank hiding behind the kitchen door. She just gathered up all her shopping bags and waddled out in a rage. Helena sobbed silently, head in hands at the table, then reached into a cupboard high above the fridge, and took out a bottle of grog.

Les had gone back into gaol after that. Another two years, for drug pushing. Frank didn't know exactly what drug pushing meant, but he knew it made the police pretty mad. Helena got quieter and quieter, and now it was as though she hardly saw Frank at all. He wondered how such a pretty mum could turn into a worn-out old woman so quickly. It must be the grog. He knew she drank herself to sleep most nights, and in the daytime she sat down quietly, staring. That was why she might let him see Dad. If he tried hard enough, maybe she wouldn't be strong enough to say no?

'Gaol is no place for a boy, Franko. I said no.'

'But, Mama, it's Dad! I haven't seen him for six months!'

Helena sighed and ran a tired hand through her unwashed hair.

'That's just as well. He's no good.'

'He is so, Mama! I love him!'

Helena smiled bitterly. 'Don't love him. He'll ruin your life like he's ruined your mother's.'

'Please let me go, Mama – please.'

'Leave your Mama alone, Franko. I'm tired.'

'Please, Mama! Please!'

Helena leaned back and closed her eyes. They'd had this conversation so often. The persistence

15

of her eight-year-old son sapped her of all her energy. She simply couldn't battle any longer.

'All right, all right. You won't give me any peace until I say yes. He's bad for you, Franko. A bad man. But if you want to, you can see him. We'll go tomorrow.'

'Yaah! Thank you, Mama!' Frank planted an excited kiss on his mother's lined cheek, and raced off to his bedroom. Helena watched him go listlessly. She knew Les was no good for Frank, but if it made the boy happy, and it kept him quiet, well, she didn't have the energy to fight. She closed her eyes and leaned back against the wall.

Alone in his dank little room, Frank pulled a large scrapbook out from beneath his bed. Grinning from ear to ear, he opened it wide. He couldn't believe he was actually going to see his dad tomorrow!

He turned the first page and read aloud: 'Man Charged with Service Station Robbery.' There was a photo of his dad underneath, with a caption that read: 'Les Morgan, 27, of Rendale.'

He knew these pages off by heart, but his eyes still widened with delight as he turned them. A catalogue of Les' criminal exploits! Burglaries, break and enters, assault charges, and the biggest one, the drug pushing story. There'd been a whole page in the paper about that. Frank guessed it must be something pretty big, because it seemed to make the police madder than most crimes. More proof that Les was the bravest and the best!

Les had started the scrapbook six years ago. Often he sat down with Frank, poring over its black and white pages, and filling his son with fanciful tales about his illegal adventures. Helena didn't like the scrapbook, so they waited until she'd gone shopping or decided to have a rest in her room. They were Frank's favourite times, those times he and Les spent together, gloating over his criminal record. Even if his dad did hit him sometimes, it was worth it. Anyway, Les was a hero, and heroes had hot tempers. Everyone knew that.

Frank turned to the last page, gazing down at a photograph of Les and Helena's wedding. She was so beautiful, so full of smiles. Frank could hardly believe this laughing lady was his listless mum of today. He wondered what it must have been like when Les and Helena were younger . . .

Helena Niarchos was a beautiful girl of eighteen when she met the ruggedly handsome Les Morgan at a local town hall dance. She was immediately attracted to his rough and ready masculinity, and for his part, he was completely entranced with her olive beauty and innocence.

Helena's parents, Spiro and Maria, owned the local delicatessen. They disliked Les Morgan right from the start, and refused to give their blessing to the brawny young Australian. Helena accused them of prejudice, saying they'd expected her to marry a Greek. They had to admit that may have been part of it, but there was something else too – something they couldn't put their finger on. As Maria told Spiro countless times, 'I don't trust the boy. I don't know why, but I think he will make our Helena's life very very unhappy.'

Helena, like all young people in love, refused to listen. She joyfully married the handsome young man who'd told her he managed a cleaning service. It wasn't until they'd been married a year and Helena was pregnant with Frank, that she discovered Les' cleaning service was a front for a housebreaking ring. Les and his shifty mates used the service to 'case' the houses they intended to rob. Helena was appalled to discover her husband's dishonesty, but she'd made her bed and she felt she had to lie in it. She found herself trapped by her pregnancy and her lifelong belief that marriage was forever. Although Helena stood by Les, her misery grew as time went by, and now at 29, she was a desperately unhappy woman, old beyond her years.

Frank closed the scrapbook and put it back beneath his bed. He'd love to see his mother smile like that again. If only he could think of a way. But later. Right now he had more exciting things to think about – like seeing his father in gaol tomorrow! Tomorrow, tomorrow – would tomorrow ever come?

The next day dawned bright and blue, though the bleakness of the gloomy prison belied the sunshine outside. Frank and Helena were led down a narrow corridor to the Visitor's Section of the gaol. Frank looked all around him excitedly, trying to absorb every little detail to recount to the fellas later. The walls were grey and silent. The prison officers wore dark blue. They looked like policemen, but Frank knew the difference. Prison officers were known as 'screws', and the one leading them down the corridor looked pretty mean. Not mean enough to scare his dad, though. Les Morgan wasn't scared of anything.

He knew his dad would be boss of all the prisoners by now. He was always the boss, wherever he was, because he was the bravest and the smartest. And he was just down the other end of this corridor!

He looked up at his mother, walking silently beside him. She didn't seem excited like he was. She'd hardly said a word all day, and just before they left for the station he'd seen her putting a bottle of grog into her tatty bag. He wished she wouldn't do it, but how could he stop her? Maybe he should tell his dad? If Les said something she'd have to listen.

'Name please?'

A stern-looking guard with a clipboard confronted them at the end of the corridor.

'Morgan – Helena and Frank. To see Les Morgan,' said Frank's mum.

'Follow me.'

Frank gripped his mother's hand in excitement as the guard led them into a large dark room full of wooden chairs and tables. There were lots of tattooed men in prison uniform, sitting around and talking to people – visitors like Helena and Frank. To Frank they seemed infinitely glamorous, men who were brave enough to risk everything for the thrill of adventure. He looked from one prisoner to the other, wondering which ones were in his dad's gang. Who were Les' best friends in here? Probably nearly everyone.

'Stop staring, Franko!' Helena pulled at his arm. 'Just sit down quietly with me.'

'I'll get Mr Morgan,' said the 'screw', as Frank and Helena sat themselves down at one of the large wooden tables. Frank's eyes followed him to the door. He couldn't believe that when he came back, he'd have Les Morgan with him! There were butterflies in his tummy as he looked around the room. He was the only kid here! Just wait 'til he told Mickey and the gang!

'Frankie Boy!'

Les was striding to the table to sit with Helena and Frank.

'Dad!' cried Frank excitedly.

The 'screw' kept his hand on Les' arm 'til they reached Helena and Frank. Les shrugged it off, saying, 'Give us a break, Ellis, I'm not goin' to rip the place apart.'

He kissed Helena and reached over to shake Frank's little hand. Frank was so proud, he thought he'd burst.

'So, how ya both been?' asked Les. Then he frowned and shook his head. 'It's not like I'm not pleased to see ya, Frank, but what are ya doin' bringin' the kid here, Helena? It's no place for a kid.'

'I'm not a kid!' cried Frank. 'I'm all grown-up!'

'Yeah? Then how come you're still about two foot tall?'

'He made me let him, Les,' said Helena nervously. 'He wouldn't give me any peace until I said he could come.'

'Yeah? You misbehavin' on your mum are ya?'

Frank just smiled and stuck his chest out. He knew Les was proud when he misbehaved. It meant his son was no wimp. Frank could hardly wait to grow up and be just like his dad. He'd come to prison too, and spend his time playing cards with his buddies and planning brand new crimes to commit.

Les didn't wait for an answer. He turned to Helena.

'You're not still hittin' the bottle are ya?'

'No, No,' said Helena defensively. 'No not me.'

'You better not be. Or I'll have to teach you a lesson.'

'I told you – I'm not!'

Frank pretended not to listen. He didn't want his mum in trouble. Anyway, she didn't know he knew.

'There's a coffee machine over there.' Helen got to her feet hurriedly. 'I'm getting one. You want one Les?'

'Yeah. No sugar.'

22

She got up quickly and walked away. Frank was thrilled to be alone with his father.

'They your mates Dad? All the fellas in here?'

'You bet, Frankie. When I say jump they say how high? I'm the boss around here. Not only the prisoners either. I'm the boss of the 'screws' too.'

'I wish I lived in here too. I will one day.'

Les threw back his head and laughed loudly.

'Yeah, sure! What would you know? You're just a kid.'

'No I'm not!'

'Yeah you are. Don't matter. Everyone's a kid sometime.'

Frank was furious. He wasn't a little boy! He quickly thought of a way to prove it.

'Me and the fellas are goin' to rob a bank, Dad!'

Les threw back his head and roared again.

'When? In fifteen years?'

'No. Tomorra.'

'A bunch of kids hardly outa nappies are goin' to rob a bank, are they?'

'We got it all planned Dad. We're gonna –'

'Don't make me laugh, kid!'

'It's for real! What we're goin' to do is –'

'You've been readin' too many nursery rhymes. There's only a few of us who really know how to do it.'

'I know how! Honest! I'm goin' to –'

'Shut-up. Your mum's comin' back!'

Helena returned with two cups of coffee and the rest of the visit passed very quickly. Frank didn't say much. He was too upset about the way his father had laughed at him. He sat there brooding over how to prove that he could pull off a real bank robbery. He'd do it, and he'd do it tomorrow, if it was the last thing he ever did!

When they got home he went to bed early. Helena didn't notice. She was sitting in front of the TV with half a bottle of gin. Frank had big plans to make – lots of things to work out. Tomorrow would become the famous day when Frank Morgan became a bank robber! He curled up in bed, dreaming about being in gaol with his father and his criminal cronies. He'd tell them all about the robbery, and Dad would be so proud that his son was brainy and brave enough to pull off a job like that. They'd probably all plan crimes together . . .

Through the thin wall Frank heard muffled sobs. Long and desperate. Quiet and hopeless.

If he was living with his dad in gaol, he wouldn't have to worry about hearing Helena cry. He wouldn't have to watch her hit the bottle, forget to make dinner, and lie around the house all day in her ragged nightie. He could escape all that, be part of a gang.

He stared up at his bedroom ceiling. Tomorrow was definitely the day!

chapter two

'Are you awake?'

'Uh–huh.'

Tom Fletcher pulled his wife Pippa towards him. She snuggled into his chest with a sigh.

'Thinking about the big day eh?'

She smiled up at him.

'Well, weren't you?'

Tom grinned, lovingly brushing a stray strand of hair from Pippa's face. 'Yeah. Of course. I still find it a bit hard to believe, Bobby and Frank getting married.'

Pippa nodded.

'I know what you mean. Kids yesterday, husband and wife the next.'

Tom squeezed his wife's shoulder.

'Feeling a bit sad about losing them?'

26

'A bit,' Pippa admitted. 'But when I think of how far they've come since we first met them . . .'

'Especially Frank.'

Pippa grinned. 'Especially Frank. A pint-sized bank robber, no less!'

'Tom! Pippa!' called a childish voice from the hallway. 'Can I come in?'

Before Tom and Pippa had time to reply, their bedroom door burst open with a flourish and their nine-year-old foster daughter Sally charged in.

'Speaking of pint-sized . . .' Tom whispered.

'What is it, darling?' asked Pippa.

'I can't sleep. I'm too excited about being Bobby and Frank's bridesmaid! Can I get in bed with you – please?'

'You know that's not allowed, Sal . . .' said Tom with mock severity.

Sally's face fell. Pippa nudged Tom in the ribs.

'But seeing it's a special day, we'll make an exception this once,' Tom finished.

'Goody!' Sally beamed broadly as she clambered into bed beside them.

'We're pretty excited too,' smiled Pippa.

Sally sighed and settled back against the pillows.

'I wish I was old enough to get married!'

'Don't even talk about it!' Pippa hugged her. 'I want at least one baby left.'

'I'm not a baby!'

'I'm sorry, sweetheart. Of course you're not.'

'You'll be getting married before we know what hit us,' said Tom.

'I hope so. I want to wear a long white dress.' She grinned. 'I love my green bridesmaid's dress, but I want to wear a bride's one too.' Suddenly Sally paused, looking from Tom to Pippa mischievously. 'Umm, you've known Frank since he was younger than me, haven't you?'

'Yep,' replied Tom. 'Since he was eight.'

'Remember what you told me a few years ago?'

Tom and Pippa exchanged a wry glance. What was Sally getting at?

'What was that Sal?' asked Pippa.

'Well when I asked you why Frank came to live with you when he was a little boy, you said I wasn't old enough to know.'

'You weren't,' said Tom.

28

Sally looked at Pippa imploringly. 'But that was a long time ago. If I'm old enough to be bridesmaid I'm old enough to know now.'

Tom and Pippa exchanged a troubled glance. Should they tell their smallest child what Frank had been like all those years ago?

'Please, Tom. Please, Pippa. Please?'

Tom shrugged his shoulders, then Pippa shrugged hers. They smiled their happy smiles that always made Sally feel safe.

'All right. I suppose you're a mature young lady now.'

Sally was delighted at the compliment.

Pippa wrapped her arm around her. She settled in for a good story-telling session.

'Well, would you believe that Frank was brought to us because he'd been caught robbing a bank?'

Sally's eyes widened with disbelief. 'Frank – robbing a bank?! You're fibbing!'

'No we're not Sal,' grinned Tom. 'He was a real little ruffian. He robbed a bank all right.'

Sally was boggle-eyed. 'But he was only eight years old! How could a little boy rob a bank?'

'Easy! It'll be a cinch!' eight year old Frank told

29

Mickey, Grub and Sam as they huddled in a corner at the end of the lane. 'Dad and all his mates in gaol'll wish they were the ones who thought of it!'

'What are ya goin' to do?' asked Grub.

'It's not what I'm goin' to do,' cried Frank. 'It's what we're goin' to do! We'll be famous! We'll be the youngest bank robbers ever. And we'll have millions of bucks to spend. We could run away! Or maybe we could pay someone to spring Dad and his mates out of gaol?!'

'But what if we got caught?' Grub was worried.

'We won't,' said Frank breezily. 'But even if we did, they'd let us off 'cause we're just kids.'

'Yeah!' Mickey was wide-eyed with excitement. 'But how will we do it? What's the plan, Morgan?'

'You guys don't have to do much,' explained Frank. 'I'll do most of the work. You just keep 'em busy at the front of the bank while I go in and rob the manager – make him hand over all the dough. Then I sneak out and we make a getaway. It'll be easy as anything!'

Sam spoke for the first time.

'But how will you make the bank manager give you the money? He'll just laugh at you 'cause you're a kid.'

Frank smiled mysteriously.

'Nobody'll be laughin' at us, I can tell you. I've got somethin' that'll make the bank manager take notice! He'll be givin' me all the money for sure. He'll be real scared.'

Mickey's eyes were like saucers.

'What is it Morgan? Watcha got?!'

'You'll find out tomorra, when we do the heist.' He looked into the intrigued eyes of his three buddies. 'Are you in it with me?'

Grub gazed down at the ground, strewn with discarded cigarette papers and aging ice cream wrappers. He fidgeted awkwardly.

'Oh, I can't Morgan. My dad'd kill me. And Gino might bash me up or somethin'.'

Frank couldn't believe his ears.

'But you're always sayin' we've gotta do a big crime!'

'Yeah, I know, but . . . my dad'd skin me alive.'

'You're chicken in other words!' yelled Frank in disgust. He turned to Sam. 'What about you, Greeno? You'll be in it.'

Sam gave his sad smile. 'I wanna, but if we get caught we'll get taken away, and I've gotta look after me grandma.' Then he too looked down at his shoes, frightened of Frank's displeasure.

Frank was staggered. This was the first time Sam had ever said no. What was going wrong? What was happening to the gang?

'Well too bad! You two missed out!' Frank screamed. 'You're just chickens! That's what you are!'

'Yeah! Chickens!' shouted Mickey. 'I'll help you, Morgan!'

'Knew I could count on you, Mickey!' cried Frank. 'Let's get out of here. Who wants to hang around with a pair of chickens?'

'Yeah!' enthused Mickey. 'Who wants to hang around with a pair of chickens?!'

They ran around Sam and Grub in circles, flapping their arms like feathery wings and screaming, 'Brrrrk – brrrkkk – brrrrk,' and other chicken calls. Then they ran away, Frank calling behind him, 'You'll be jealous when we're on TV!'

'Yeah! We'll show ya, ya scaredy-cat babies!' called Mickey. And they disappeared around a corner, leaving Sam and Grub looking after them, ashamed.

Later that night, when his mum thought he was

outside playing, Frank slipped in her bedroom window and tiptoed to her bed. He knew he'd be pretty safe, because Helena had been drinking again and she didn't see or hear very much when she was drunk. But still he moved quietly and stealthily. He couldn't let his mum find out he was reaching under her bed for – a gun!

He held the revolver in his little hands, then pointed it at the mirror. It was Les' gun. His mum didn't know he knew about it, but one night he'd heard them having a fight. Mum had said 'You can't have a gun in the house with a child nearby!' and Les had said 'Relax Helena, a bloke never knows when he might need a bit of help. But if you're worried about the kid, I won't keep no bullets in it. All right?'

Helena had agreed reluctantly. 'All right. But don't ever tell Frankie it's here.'

'Okay, I won't. Now will ya stop naggin' me?'

Les had never told Frank about the gun, but he didn't have to, because Frank had heard everything! He pretended to fire. Pow! Pow! Pow! Frank had always known that one day the gun would come in handy, but he hadn't known that day would arrive so quickly. Tomorrow! And even though Frank knew the gun wasn't loaded, the bank manager wouldn't know that, and he'd hand over all of his dough quick smart!

Frank smiled as he sneaked back to his room. Wait 'til his father heard about the robbery! He wouldn't think Frank was a little kid then! Maybe they could roam the country together like the Kelly gang did a hundred years ago? All for one and one for all! Him and his dad would live on the road, robbing nasty rich people and being kind to poor ones. They'd buy his mum pretty dresses and jewels, and she'd stop drinking and staring into space and start cooking yummy meals like roast dinners with apple pie.

'You in there, Frankie?'

Frank hurriedly stuffed the gun under his blankets.

'Yeah, Mum.'

'Good. It's too dark for playing outside. You go to sleep like a little boy should – okay?' she called through the door.

'Okay, Mama.'

Frank heard her walking slowly down the hall-way towards her room. He quickly pulled the gun out from under the blankets and hid it beneath his bed. After tomorrow he'd be able to buy his mother anything she wanted. Maybe he could buy her one of those bright coloured dresses he'd seen in department store windows? He'd be rich! He grinned. Him and Mickey. Rich and brave. Wait 'til Mickey saw the gun!

But Mickey's reaction the next day was very different to what Frank had imagined.

'Watcha doin', Morgan? Where'd ya get that?!'

His face was a picture of terror as Frank took the gun out from under a jumper.

'It's Dad's. They don't know I know about it.'

'But what if we kill someone? What if someone kills us? We might get hurt. I didn't know you were goin' to bring a gun. I mightn't –'

'You're not goin' to be a chicken too, are ya?' Frank interrupted threateningly. 'It's not loaded. Mum wouldn't let Dad keep bullets in it. And I didn't put any in 'cause I don't know how to open it.'

Mickey still looked unconvinced.

'It's not goin' to hurt no one. It's just goin' to scare the bank manager into givin' us the dough!'

Mickey gulped nervously. 'I dunno, Morgan. Maybe I better not. If me mum and dad find out, they'll kill me. I might go to gaol or somethin'.'

Frank stamped his foot on the ground impatiently. 'Look, I told ya – we're not goin' to get busted, but even if we did, they'd let us off 'cause we're only kids. You're not gettin' gutless on me are ya? Think of bein' rich and famous! You could buy your dad a new car! You don't have to do anything except keep 'em busy anyway. I'm the one who's gonna be pointin' the gun!'

Mickey shuffled nervously. Frank panicked. He couldn't do it on his own.

'I thought you were me best mate. The only one who didn't let me down.'

Mickey was silent for another moment, then he smiled and held out his hand to shake. 'Yeah. All right. I'll do it.'

'Good on ya!' yelled Frank, shaking his mate's hand vigorously. 'Let's go show the bank manager who's boss!'

They turned on their heels and started striding towards the bank they'd decided to target. This was it. Their first big job! The two little boys had everything planned. The robbery would run as smooth as silk. In a couple of hours they'd be heroes!

Frank pulled a large men's handkerchief from a pocket in his ragged shorts. 'See this? It's me dad's. I'll wear it as a mask. The manager won't be able to give a description to the cops then.'

Mickey stared at the hanky in puzzlement. 'But how will you be able to see, man?'

'You tie it under your eyes, stupid,' snorted Frank, 'not on top of 'em! Haven't you seen those western movies on TV?'

'Oh yeah,' Mickey laughed in embarrassment. 'I forgot.'

They turned a corner and it loomed ahead. The bank. Just 100 metres away. Frank felt a whole flock of butterflies invade his tummy. He knew Mickey was scared, but he was determined not to let his mate find out he was frightened too. They stopped on the corner to finalize the plan.

'Right? You know what you've gotta do?' he asked Mickey firmly.

'Yeah – what we worked out yesterday. I'm scared but.'

'Don't be scared. I'm not,' Frank lied. 'It'll be a cinch. Once the manager sees the gun he'll be handin' over the dough so quick we'll be outa there in twenty seconds. Just don't act suspicious.'

'Okay,' gulped Mickey, petrified. And they walked towards the bank.

As they arrived at the entrance they stared inside. There were about ten people standing in queues, waiting to see a teller. And there seemed to be six people or so working behind the counter. Frank was frightened by the sight of so many grown-ups, but he was determined to go through with it. He knew the gun would do the trick, even though it wasn't loaded.

Mickey was as white as a ghost as Frank pushed the bank door open. A few people glanced up, then looked away again. Nobody took much notice of the two scruffy little boys. They all assumed they were with someone else.

Frank beckoned for Mickey to stay where he was, while he cased the joint for the manager's office. There it was – at the back of the bank! A door with the words 'Bank Manager' written in bold gold letters. The door was ajar. Frank gulped. His heart felt like it was going to explode, but there was no turning back now. He turned and nodded to Mickey, who looked sick with terror.

Almost immediately Mickey started clutching his tummy and screaming out in pretend agony. 'Oh my stomach! My appendix! Oh oh! It hurts! Where's my mum? I can't walk! I can't walk!' Mickey collapsed in a heap on the floor, as several people descended on him, anxious to help the little boy in distress. Staff and customers rushing to Mickey's aid as he lay on the ground, moaning and groaning.

Quick as a wink Frank slid behind the counter,

and tying the hanky around his face, hurried to the Bank Manager's office. His heart was beating a hundred to the dozen as he pushed the door open and rushed inside, closing it behind him. He pulled the gun out from under the jumper and pointed it at the middle aged man who sat at the desk, staring in amazement.

'What's all the racket about?' he was asking in annoyance as Frank came charging into the room. Then the door slammed shut and his attention was taken by the pint-sized robber who stood before him, checked hankie obscuring his features, gun pointed straight ahead with hands that shook like leaves.

'What's going on here?' demanded the bank manager. 'Who are you, young man?'

Frank took a sharp breath and tried in vain to stop the gun shaking. He spoke in the deepest voice he could muster. 'Hand over the money and nobody gets hurt.'

There was a stunned silence and then, to Frank's fury, the bank manager actually laughed. 'I think you've been watching a few too many movies, son. Why don't you just run off home? I'm a busy man with a lot of work to do.'

He was laughing, making fun of Frank just like his father had. Everyone treated him like a baby.

Well he'd show the lot of them! 'I said – hand over the money! Or I'll shoot that smile right off your face!'

But the bank manager still smiled. He leaned across the desk and looked at Frank's gun.

'It's a very convincing toy, but you're running the risk of getting into serious trouble here. What if I told your parents about this incident?'

'It's not a toy! It's a real gun! So watch out! Now give me the money!'

In Frank's blind panic, he unconsciously squeezed the trigger of the gun. Why wouldn't the bank manager take him seriously? Why did everybody think he was funny?

'I'm not giving you any money,' said the bank manager. 'And the joke's wearing thin. Now if I were you, little boy –'

'It's not a joke – and I'm not a little boy!' Frank screamed in fury. He squeezed the trigger hard without realizing, and all of a sudden the air was shattered with an almighty bang. The gun was loaded! It fell from his hands. Frank gaped at the hole he'd shot in the wall behind the bank manager's desk, then turned around and ran for his life.

'What's going on? What was that?!'

'It was a gunshot!'

'Oh my God! Is Mr Wilson all right?!'

Complete chaos broke out in the bank as Frank sprinted for the door, yelling, 'Get out, Mickey! Make a break for it!'

Mickey leapt to his feet and the two little boys ran like rockets into the busy street, eluding all the grown-ups who were screaming out angrily, 'Catch them! Get those little terrors! Where are their parents?! Call the police!'

Frank had always been a faster runner than Mickey, and soon he was quite a few metres ahead. 'Hurry up, Mickey! Hurry up!' he screamed. He sprinted as though being chased by the devil. The next time he looked over his shoulder he saw a young patrol policeman hot on Mickey's trail! 'Move, Mickey! Move!!!' But it was too late! The young policeman leapt into the air and grabbed Mickey's ankles in a rugby league tackle. Frank ran on, made fast by fear, and disappeared around a corner. The cops had Mickey! What would happen now?

Several hours later, as night came closer, a grubby little boy emerged from behind a pile of old cardboard boxes at the rear of a fruit and vegetable store. Frank was shivering, not from cold, but from fright. What would happen to

Mickey? Was he all right? Did they lock him up?
Did they hurt him? Frank stretched and tried to
stifle a tear. His small body was stiff from crouch-
ing in amongst the boxes all afternoon. The air
was thick with the smell of rotting fruit, and
maggots hovered above over-ripe peaches,
thrown out by the shopkeeper.

Frank turned to start trudging home. It didn't
seem exciting now. None of it. Not any more. It
was scary and horrible, and stupid too. He didn't
want to be a bank robber any more. He just
wanted to be at home with his mum. As he
approached their dingy street, he thought of
Helena. Not the way she was now, but the way
she was once. He wished with all his heart that
when he got home she would gather him up in
her strong young arms and call him her 'agapimu' like she used to. He wished she'd sing him
those funny old songs, tell him some silly stories,
and smile down at him again, with her hair
falling in soft dark waves to her shoulders. Maybe
if he asked her properly she'd let him sleep with
her tonight? He didn't feel like a brave criminal.
He felt like a frightened, confused little boy.

Clutching those dreams to his heart, he turned
the corner into his street, and looked for the
reassuring sight of his mother's decrepit terrace
house. Suddenly he stopped in his tracks. Helena
was out the front of the house, talking to – a

policeman! As he stood there wondering what to do, his mother saw him and called his name.

'Franko! Run! Franko!'

The policeman was on the chase in an instant. Frank turned and fled, tripping around the corner and knocking over a metal garbage bin as he tried to make good his escape. The long-legged policeman wasn't far behind. He quickly closed the gap between them. It looked like he would catch Frank up, 'til Frank turned a sudden corner, twisted through a broken fence; and ran like fury into a viaduct, where he'd hidden from his father's rages and his mother's drinking binges many times in the past. The policemen followed him in, but Frank knew a great hiding place – a little crevice in the viaduct wall a bit further along. If he hid in there, the policeman's torch couldn't even find him. He tripped down the dark viaduct 'til he found the small crevice. He sank into a little huddle, breathing in heaving gasps. He'd shaken them off again! There's no way they'd catch him here.

A torch shone brightly into his eyes. He blinked, trying to regain his vision, then stared into the face of the policeman. Oh, no! It was Constable Carmichael from the local police station. He'd had harsh words with Frank and the gang before, about window breaking and vandalism.

chapter two

Constable Carmichael shook his head with a grim smile.

'Well, Frank. You've really done it this time!'

Frank gulped. He was still almost blinded by the torchlight.

'You've had more than enough chances. Well, no more. We'll have to take you away this time.'

He pulled Frank to his feet and led him out of the viaduct. Frank shuffled silently beside him, head down, battling tears. They must be taking him to gaol . . . into a grey, lonely cell where all he'd ever see would be black steel bars that separated him from Mickey and the gang, from the rest of the world, from Mum. He held back hot tears. 'Don't be such a wimpo,' he told himself. 'It'll be great, being in gaol. You can hang around with Dad. Maybe they'll put you in the cell next door? You can play cards together and plan more crimes. Beats staying at home and watching Mum become a stranger, like a ghost or a person who isn't even there. Better than wishing things be like they used to be, but secretly knowing they never will be. Yeah. It'd have to be better than that. Living in gaol with Dad will be great.'

But Constable Carmichael didn't take Frank to gaol. He took him to a place called Meringale

Children's Home, where ladies like teachers fed
him chops and potatoes; and put him to bed in a
big room full of other kids, where the sheets
were white and crispy clean. They didn't tell
him what was going to happen, and Frank didn't
ask. He was so tired all of a sudden. Tired of
trying to be so tough, tired of pretending to be
grown-up, tired of being sad about his mum, tired
of having to fend for himself. Just for tonight, he
didn't care what happened. He didn't want to
know.

The confused, vulnerable little boy fell asleep
almost instantly.

'You gonna send me to gaol?'

The next morning Frank's rebelliousness
returned. He wanted to go back to his mum,
back to the gang, back to the secret hideout in
the little lane behind Wilson Street. But they
were acting like he couldn't – these teacher
ladies and social workers, and even a lady policeman, who wore black lace-up shoes like school
ones. They said he mightn't be going back there
for a long time. He was going to a Children's
Court, and then he was probably going to live
somewhere new.

'You're too young to go to gaol,' said one of the
ladies, whose name was Mrs Hill.

'Then where am I goin'?'

'You're going to live with some nice, happy people.'

Frank was angry. What were they talking about? He belonged with his mum. 'I don't want to live with some nice, happy people.'

'We'll find a family who'll be just right,' said Mrs Hill.

'Don't wanna go!' he yelled.

But they didn't care about what he wanted. They took him to a place called The Children's Court and an old-looking magistrate asked him stupid questions about Helena and Les. Then they told him to wait outside with the lady policeman. Frank sat in the corridor silently, refusing the policewoman's offer of a fizzy drink or a vegemite sandwich. She tried to put her arm around him, but he shrugged it off angrily. And then, after a little while, the courtroom door opened, and out stepped – his mother!

'Mama! Mama!' Frank tore like a torpedo down the corridor, screaming with joy. He threw himself into Helena's arms, crying 'Take me home, Mama, take me home!'

Helena wrapped her thin arms around Frank, tears streaming down her colourless cheeks. She stroked his soft hair, her voice heavy with weary regret. 'I'm sorry, Franko, I'm sorry . . .'

Frank's breath caught in his throat. He panicked. What was his mother talking about?

'They're right, Franko, they're right.' Her voice trembled. 'You're better off with somebody else . . .'

'No, Mama! No!!!' He hid his face in her chest.

'I'm sorry, Franko,' she repeated with infinite sadness. 'I'm too tired, I'm just too tired . . . I can't do it no more, I can't . . .'

As Frank clung to her with little fists clenched white in desperation, she looked to the lady policeman for help. The policewoman gently pulled Frank away. He barely noticed that her face was also wet with tears. 'No, Mama no!' he sobbed. 'Don't go!'

Helena reached down and kissed his forehead. 'It's for the best. I'm no good . . .'

'Yes you are!'

'They'll get you a proper family . . . be good, Franko, be good . . .'

And as the policewoman held a numb Frank back, Helena walked away. Sobbing silently, the fragile young mother left her son's childhood behind.

chapter three

'Here comes the bride, here comes the bride!'

Celia Stewart hummed the age-old Wedding March as she fussed around the general store, doing a spot of tidying up before closing down for the wedding. There was no point in staying open today. After all, anyone who was anyone would be at the church!

How Celia loved a wedding! They were always so moving, so joyful – the union of two young lives forever more. She sighed wistfully. Even if the bride was Bobby Simpson.

Oh, Celia had nothing against Bobby, of course. She was quite a decent young girl beneath that unfortunately tough exterior. But she had always hoped that one day her handsome young tenant, Frank, and her niece, Ruth, might be reunited. Of course, it would have been difficult after all that unfortunate business with the baby, Ruth's unwise deception, and then Frank's accident; but still, they surely could have overcome

those problems and lived happily ever after. Celia
was convinced of it. But alas, it seemed that was
not to be. She shook her head in puzzlement.
What young man could possibly prefer the tom-
boyish Bobby to the beautiful Ruth?

She was still pondering this question when her
old school chum and Ladies Auxiliary com-
panion, Betty Falwell, raced in the door at a
hundred miles an hour.

'Celia, dear – you won't believe it! I bought a
lovely new pink frock for the wedding and a
stylish pink handbag to match, but I didn't remember to buy pink pantyhose! I don't know
what I could have been thinking of!'

'Well, the pantyhose rack is over there, dear,'
pointed Celia.

'I know that,' said Betty, miffed. 'I buy them
here each time don't I?'

Celia dusted off the shelves as Betty flicked
through the pantyhose packets. 'It seems everyone has bought themself a new outfit for the big
day, Betty.'

'Well, one can't attend a wedding in an old
frock, can one?' replied Betty, carrying her
chosen pantyhose to the counter.

'Indeed not,' agreed Celia. She took Betty's

money and rang up the till. 'There must be quite some excitement at the Fletchers this morning!'

'My word yes!' twittered Betty. 'With little Sally a bridesmaid.'

'And Carly, of course,' Celia reminded her confidante.

'Well, sometimes I think the less said about that young lady the better,' sighed Betty. 'A life fraught with so many problems.' She lowered her voice and looked around to make certain no one else was present. 'Especially this latest drinking business. She's certainly given the Fletchers a run for their money, hasn't she?'

Celia leaned across the counter confidentially. 'So has the bride, in the past.'

'My word yes! What a little ruffian Bobby was!' agreed Betty. She pondered the point for a moment. 'Tom and Pippa are to be praised for their charity in taking on those children. It can't have been easy.'

'Oh, Betty you don't know the half of it, my dear!' Celia replied conspiratorially. 'The trauma poor Tom and Pippa went through with young Frank when he was barely out of the cradle would try the patience of a saint!'

Betty frowned. 'I've never heard about this, Celia.

50

You mean to say you've known about Frank's troubled childhood all this time and never said a word to your best friend about it?'

Celia put her hand to her chest in indignation. 'Betty, dear, what do you think I am? A gossip?'

Celia hurried to the door and shut it, flipping the sign over to CLOSED. She invited Betty to take a seat, then sat down beside her friend. 'When Frank was a little waif,' she whispered, 'he spent his first weeks with Tom and Pippa planning a brazen escape!'

Betty's eyes widened.

Frank lay in bed, staring skywards. Boy, oh boy, check out that stupid mobile with elephants and bright yellow tigers hanging off the ceiling. How old did these Tom and Pippa turkeys think he was? Three? Huh! Tom and Pippa! – what stupid names anyway. He remembered when he'd first met them, about a month ago. They'd arrived at his temporary foster home to take him on a picnic. She had blonde hair and looked like a pixie. He was a wimp. Frank could tell a mile off. He knew they were supposed to be his new foster parents, so he gave them a real hard time. Weird thing was, they seemed to like him anyway. They kept taking him out for the day and asking him to stay overnight. Then about three weeks ago, he'd moved to their place for good.

Well, they thought he was here for good anyway, but Frank knew better! There was no way he was going to stay with these dags. He had it all worked out. Pretty soon they wouldn't see him for dust!

He looked around at the other toys Tom and Pippa had bought him over the weeks. An electric train set, a couple of model aeroplanes, and a football – a plastic football?!

What was it with them? Didn't they know he wasn't interested in kid's toys, or this room they'd freshly painted for him? A couple of weeks ago Pippa had asked his favourite colours. He'd said blue and red just to get her off his back, even though he did kind of like those colours. And Tom had gone and painted his bedroom red and blue all over! What a pair of goody-goody crawlers! It took more than a coat of paint to win Frank Morgan over. And all their stupid games! The wimpy little kids they knew might like them, but Frank had better things to do with his time.

He thought back to life as it used to be up 'til the day of the failed bank robbery. It was great, roaming the streets any time day or night without anyone telling him what to do, or hassling him to come home for his dinner. If he went out to play after 5.30pm these days, little Frogface (his nickname for Pippa) nearly chucked a fit. She thought something might happen to him. Huh! Didn't she know he could look after himself? He'd been doing it for ages, ever since Mum had started drinking. He was used to looking after himself. That was the way he liked it.

And Tom and Pippa expected him to tell them all about school. What was to tell? His new school was the same every day. Off. Full of creepy crawlers and brainy kids. Why should he have to spill his guts to them about his stupid lessons? He'd never had to with his mum or dad.

Never mind, he told himself. Today's the day to get out of this hole! He'd been planning it for two weeks now. He knew the perfect way to escape, but it had to be today! He'd show these turkeys he wasn't some sooky kid. Before they knew what hit them he'd be off, and they'd never find him.

'Frank, time to get up,' Frogface called, knocking on his bedroom door. 'Get dressed for school and I'll get your breakfast ready, all right?'

Frank ignored her. She waited a moment, then called again.

'Frank, time to get up!'

'I heard ya the first time!' he snarled through the door. There was silence for a moment, then the door opened, and Tom, or Wimphead as Frank thought of him, came into the room. Frank could tell he was angry. Suck eggs!

'There's no need to speak to Pippa like that,' said Wimphead. 'Now do as she says and get up, eh?'

'All right, all right,' Frank snapped sulkily. He climbed slowly out of bed. He knew Wimphead wanted to yell at him, but Frogface silenced him with a look.

'We'll see you at breakfast in ten minutes,' she smiled. They went out closing the door behind them, leaving Frank to get dressed in his daggy school uniform.

Fifteen minutes later Frank sat in sullen silence at the breakfast table. He ignored Tom and Pippa's repeated attempts to draw him into conversation.

'Will you pass me the salt please Frank?' asked Frogface.

He pretended not to hear her request. She raised her eyebrows at Wimphead.

'Pippa said will you pass her the salt?' said Wimphead grimly.

Frank was fed-up with these two jerk-brains telling him what to do. 'What's the matter with her? Hasn't she got hands of her own?'

Wimphead threw his fork down. It clattered with a bang on the pine table top. 'Now listen here, son, I've had just about as much as –'

'Leave it, Tom,' interrupted Frogface. 'I'll get the salt for myself.' She reached over and picked up the salt, then sprinkled it over her bacon and eggs. There was silence for a moment.

'What's happening at school today, Frank?' she asked.

'Nothin'. What's it to you anyway?'

Again Wimphead was forced to restrain himself by a powerful warning glance from Frogface.

'I was talking to Miss Flannery yesterday and she said your class was having a birthday party for one of the girls this afternoon.'

'She don't know what she's talkin' about.'

'That's it!' yelled Wimphead. 'I will not have you speaking to Pippa in that manner. Apologise immediately.'

Frank was silent.

'I said apologise.'

Still Frank said nothing.

'You're not leaving this room until you say sorry.'

Frank stared at Wimphead defiantly. He put down his knife and fork, pulled his chair back from the table, stood up and walked out of the kitchen, slamming the door behind him. He heard Wimphead say 'I'm trying as hard as I can to be patient, Pip, but what that boy needs is a good hiding.'

Huh! thought Frank. I'll tell ya what I need. To get away from jerks like you. And that's exactly what I'm goin' to do. After this afternoon, I'll be history! He picked up his school bag, tied his shoelaces, and ran from the house, pulling the front door shut with a bang!

In the kitchen, Tom Fletcher gave a loud gasp of exasperation. 'How'd you like that? Not so much as a "See you later." As I said Pip, I feel sorry for the kid, but we can only take so much. And I'm telling you – I've had a gutful!'

Pippa sighed as she munched on a piece of toast. 'I know. He can be a little terror.'

'Can be?!' scoffed Tom. 'He is every minute of the day.' He thought for a moment. 'I don't like to admit defeat, but maybe we're not cut out for this? We don't seem to be doing the kid any good so far.'

'You can't give up already, Tom,' Pippa reasoned.
'The Department warned us it would be like this.
It takes a long time to gain someone's trust –
especially a frightened little boy who's used to
being mistreated.' She reached over and took
her husband's hand. 'Think about it. The poor
kid's never been able to rely on anyone before.
He's not going to let his guard down in a hurry,
is he? For all he knows, we're going to up and
run or decide we don't care. He's terrified of
getting close to us. We've just got to give him
time. Show him we do care and it's not just a
temporary thing.'

Tom smiled lovingly at his pretty young wife.
'So much wisdom in one so beautiful. You're
right of course, as usual.' He kissed the top of
Pippa's head as he got up from the table. 'It's
just that sometimes I could cheerfully wring his
scrawny little neck.'

'I know the feeling,' Pippa grinned. 'But toler-
ance is the key, remember?'

'Yes, Sir!' smiled Tom; as he took a couple of
notes from his wallet. 'Here's this week's shopping money. Will I put it in the usual place?'
Pippa nodded. Tom walked over to the sideboard
and slipped the money inside an ornamental
teapot. 'Never let it be said I'm not a tolerant
man, but at the same time, I'm not stupid. So

don't let that little ratbag know where we put the shopping money, or it won't be there for long!'

'Don't be so cynical about him,' urged Pippa. 'If we don't trust him, what's he got to aim for? As long as he knows he has our trust, he'll reward us with honesty, I'm sure.'

Though Pippa spoke with every appearance of confidence, she wasn't really so certain. And later that morning, in Frank's old neighbourhood, her secret fears were confirmed . . .

'I got it all worked out!' Frank was telling Mickey. 'Every Thursday he gives her the shopping money and she puts it in this daggy old teapot. They think I don't know about it. Today's Thursday, right? She's a nurse and she does a shift at some hospital that starts at 11. So I sneak back there when she's gone to work, and pinch the dough. Easy! If you can flog some off your olds as well, we'll be set! We can run away and start a new life on the run, like on TV!'

Mickey, who was on a Good Behaviour Bond as a result of the aborted bank robbery, didn't react with his usual enthusiasm. 'No, Morgan, you do it. I'm already in enough trouble.'

'Come on, Mickey! What are ya? Gutless?!'

'Look what happened last time. I don't want to

58

get in more trouble. I don't want 'em to take me away from Mum and Dad like they did to you.'

Frank fell silent. He'd been to the old terrace house this morning, planning to walk in and surprise his mum. But the doors and windows were locked and there was no answer, no matter how loud he called out her name. And then, as he walked out the gate, he'd noticed a FOR SALE sign out the front.

'Where's my mum gone?'

Mickey stared down at the ground. 'I dunno. How would I know?'

'Have you heard your parents sayin' anything? Ask 'em. Maybe they know where she is.'

'She's gone away somewhere,' Mickey mumbled.

'Where to?'

'Dunno, but she's gone for good. I heard my Mum telling Dad.'

His mum gone for good somewhere strange and mysterious. She didn't want him anymore. He fought against the sadness that made his small heart heavy. All the more reason to opt for a life on the run. But it wouldn't be as much fun on his own. Mickey had to come with him. 'Come on, Mick – let's do it!'

Mickey shook his head. He didn't seem scared of Frank any more. 'Sorry, Morgan. Not gonna. I don't want to get in no more trouble.'

Fury rose in Frank's little heart. It seemed the whole world was against him. He couldn't rely on anyone these days, not even good old Mickey. Well good old Mickey was gutless, so Frank didn't need him any more either.

'All right, you wimp. I'll do it on my own then. Be more fun by myself anyway,' he lied. And he ran away forever, shouting 'I'll send you a post-card from Surfers Paradise!'

As Frank, sprinted through the streets he thought about life on the run. It'd be tops – just like on TV. He'd travel from city to city, never stopping long enough for anyone to recognise him. He'd dodge police barricades and hide out in aban-doned railway carriages, occasionally accepting the kindness of beautiful young women, who would smuggle him food; or rich old men who used to be criminals and admired him for his bravery. When he got old enough he'd grow a beard and wear an eyepatch as a disguise.

Back in the Fletcher's leafy suburb, hidden across the road from their house, he watched as Frog-face climbed into the car wearing her stupid nurse's uniform. She backed out of the drive slowly and carefully – what a dag! – then disappeared around the corner. Hurriedly Frank scrambled across the road and took out the spare key they'd given him. He let himself into the house, changed out of his poxy school uniform, and opened the lid of the teapot. There it was! The means of his escape! He rummaged through the 'fridge and pantry, stealing enough food to keep him going for the first few days. Then he gathered it all up in a bundle, and slipped out of the house. He started off down the street, beaming from ear to ear. He was on his way to freedom, and a lifetime of adventures!

Eight hours later, Pippa looked on anxiously as Tom hung up the telephone from Frank's new primary school.

'He wasn't there all day – the little ratbag!' snarled Tom.

'What if something's happened to him?' fretted Pippa.

'Something'll happen to him soon enough when I get hold of him!' Tom said furiously. 'I'm going to look around the streets in case he's hanging out with louts somewhere. You stay here in case he turns up.' Tom kissed Pippa goodbye and headed off.

He drove the car slowly through the suburban streets, searching the footpaths in vain for Frank.

Occasionally he cruised past groups of little boys, slowing down almost to a halt as he studied their faces for any sign of Frank. After half an hour he was forced to admit that Frank wasn't loitering in the streets – not around this area anyway. Then suddenly a thought occurred to him, and he quickly turned the car around, heading in the direction of Frank's old neighbourhood.

'What's it to ya?'

Mickey gulped nervously up at the grown-up man staring down at him. This must be the guy Frank called Wimphead – but he didn't look like a wimp to Mickey. He looked pretty tough, and he looked like he could lose his temper any minute. Mickey didn't want to be around when he did.

'The boys around the corner told me you're Frank's best mate. He hasn't been seen all day. Do you know where he is?'

Mickey feigned a toughness he didn't feel. 'Who's askin'?'

'Frank's foster father, that's who. Tom Fletcher. Please, Mickey, tell me the truth. Do you know where he is?'

Mickey shuffled from foot to foot, thinking. He didn't want to give his best mate away, but . . .

he was tired of getting in trouble with grown-ups, sick of the scrapes Frank had led him into, and most of all, he was scared that he too would be taken away from his parents. 'No, but . . .'

Tom moved forward. His face was anxious. 'But???'

Mickey felt awful. He'd started now. He knew he'd have to tell Tom everything. He just hoped that Frank would forgive him. 'He came over this mornin'. Said he was runnin' away.'

'Running away?' repeated Tom. 'We were frightened of that. Where to? Where to, Mickey?'

Mickey shook his head nervously. This Fletcher guy wouldn't hit him, would he? 'I dunno. But he said he'd send me a postcard from Surfers' Paradise.'

Tom studied the little boy's frightened face. He was obviously telling the truth. His heart went out to the miniature 'toughie' who was obviously accustomed to pretty rough treatment. He patted Mickey's shoulder. 'Okay. Thanks, mate,' he said. 'Maybe you could come over and play at our place one day when Frank gets back? Pippa'd like to meet you.' He turned around and walked away.

Mickey looked after Tom's retreating back. He didn't know why Frank said he was such a wimp. Mickey thought Tom Fletcher seemed pretty cool. He turned back to his game of marbles.

'But what would he be doing for money?' Tom puzzled, back at home with Pippa.

Pippa took the plunge, telling her husband – 'I didn't say anything before, because it would have confirmed all your worst fears, but the money in the teapot's missing.'

Tom's brow clouded over. 'That'd be right.' He sank into a chair at the kitchen table. 'Still, we'll worry about punishment when we've got him safely back here.' He scratched his head worriedly. 'What'll we do Pip? Do you think we should call in the Department of Youth and Community Services?'

Pippa shook her head emphatically. 'Maybe we should technically, but I'd rather not just yet Tom. Frank's got such a distrust of authority – he'd only resent us more. If we keep mum about things and get him back ourselves, I think we'll have a lot better chance of earning his respect.'

Tom smiled across the table at his wife. 'Right again,' he said. 'But where do you reckon we should start looking?'

Pippa puzzled for a moment. 'I don't know,' she admitted.

Tom's face lit up. He slapped his hand on the table. 'I do!' he exclaimed. 'Think about it for a sec. What area do runaway kids in the city traditionally head for?'

'Not Kings Cross?!'

Tom nodded.

Pippa was dubious. 'He's only eight years old, Tom!'

'I know,' conceded Tom, 'but hold on a tick. The poor fella likes to think he's a real tough customer, right?'

Pippa nodded with a smile. She certainly couldn't deny that!

'Where do tough customers go but the Cross!? Come on Pip, we're driving over there. You wait. I bet I'm right.'

And he was. At that moment Frank was wandering wide-eyed along the sleazy streets of Kings Cross; trying to master a devil-may-care saunter as he strolled past prostitutes lolling in doorways and loud-mouthed spruikers extolling the pleasures of every kind of perverse entertainment. He soaked in the exotic sights and sounds, dreaming of how he would conquer the Cross. Soon everyone would know him here, and they'd call out hullo from their darkened doorways as he sauntered casually by. They'd all be in awe of his toughness and bravery, and no-one would treat him like a kid.

Frank's mind was ablaze with this wonderful dream when he came to a stop outside a particularly slimy looking establishment, advertising, 'Non-Stop Erotic Entertainment.' He stood up to his full height and headed for the entrance. After all, if he was going to spend his life in the Cross, he'd have to get into the action.

'Where d'ya think you're goin', kid?'

Loud laughter belowed out above his head. He looked up into the toothless face of the spruiker. He had tattooes on his arms and a short spiky haircut. Frank decided he'd look like that when he was grown-up. He'd be tough as nuts!

'Wanna bit do ya? Ha ha!' He called out to another spruiker a few doors down: 'Hey, check it out, Davo! The kid wants to get his rocks off with our ladies upstairs!'

The slimy spruiker down the road joined in his raucous laughter. Frank felt fury rise in his chest. He was being treated like a baby – again!

'Let me in!' he yelled.

'No way, kid,' scoffed the beefy spruiker. 'We already got the cops hasslin' us enough. Ya think we're goin' to give 'em the chance to find a kid inside? Ha! Go change your nappy will ya? Buzz off!'

Frank tried to stand his ground, but the spruiker advanced menacingly, his mean-looking face looming overhead. 'It was funny for 10 seconds kid. Get lost now, or you'll be real bloody sorry!'

Frank didn't dare argue. He scuttled away hurriedly, his ears burning at the insulting guffaws that followed him down the street. He turned the corner and saw a pinball parlour a few doors down on the left. Thinking gleefully of the shopping money waiting to be spent in his pocket, he headed inside. His eyes opened wide. Every imaginable pinball game was here in this one large room. Lights flashed and machines went bing! Wow! He grinned happily. The Cross was really his kind of place.

'Out the way, jerk!'

Frank was roughly shoved aside as a rowdy group of older boys headed for a machine nearby. His temper was reaching boiling point. He'd had more than enough of being written off as some stupid kid. His frustration made him reckless.

'You get out the way!' he yelled angrily.

The older boys gathered in a circle around him, faces nasty and threatening.

.'What did you say?' demanded the toughest-looking boy, who wore a checked flannelette shirt and jeans with holes. His hair was long and greasy, and a skull and crossbones hung from his right ear. Frank gulped nervously, determined not to let these toughies see that he was frightened.

'I said you get out of the way!'

'That's what I thought you said,' sneered Skull and Crossbones. 'And who are you to tell us what to do?'

Frank took a deep breath. He was sick of being scared. He'd show these turkeys he was every bit as tough as them!

'I'm a bank robber!' he exclaimed.

His daring confession didn't have quite the effect he'd intended. The other boys laughed their heads off around him, nudging each other and snorting with scorn at the unlikely criminal.

'Check the baby who reckons he's a bank robber!' sneered Skull and Crossbones. 'Aint even old enough to wipe his snotty nose, but he reckons he can rob a bank!'

'Yeah!' jeered his adolescent companions.

'I did so rob a bank!' yelled Frank. 'And I stole money off my foster parents too! So there!'

Skull and Crossbones suddenly looked interested. He beckoned to the other boys to be quiet, and leaned over to talk to Frank. His breath smelt of cigarettes and chiko rolls. 'You stole some money off your olds eh? When?'

'This mornin',' boasted Frank.

The older boy stepped back and winked at his grimy buddies. 'Prove it, kid. If you really did it maybe I'll let you hang around with us.'

Frank reached into his jeans pocket. He'd show these guys he meant business! They'd be so impressed that before long Frank'd be boss, and Skull and Crossbones would take orders from him. When Frank said 'Jump!' he'd say 'How high?' He pulled the notes out of his pocket and held out his hand. 'See? There's –'

But he didn't get the chance to say any more, because Skull and Crossbones grabbed the money and careered out of the pinball parlour, closely followed by his laughing mates.

'Sucko, little kid! Go home to Mummy and Daddy!' yelled Skull and Crossbones.

Frank saw red. He didn't care that there were five of them. He didn't care that they were all bigger than him. The shopping money was all he had. He was going to start a new life with it. They couldn't take it from him – they wouldn't take it from him! He raced after them like a miniscule rocket, yelling out in fury 'They've got my money! Give it back, you scumbags! Give it back!!'

And that was how Tom and Pippa saw him, running through a Kings Cross street in pursuit of five boys almost twice his size.

'There he is, Tom!' cried Pippa. 'Quick! Let's get him! Hurry up! Park!'

''Struth!' Tom exclaimed in frustration as their eyes peeled the side of the street. This was the infamous Kings Cross. There wasn't a parking spot in sight!

'If we don't go after him we'll lose him!' screamed the normally tranquil Pippa. 'He went around the corner! Quick!'

Tom brought the car to a screeching halt. He undid his seat belt and threw the door open. '*You find a park* Pip. I'll follow him!'

'Those boys looked nasty!' warned Pippa as she slid hurriedly across to the driver's seat.

'Don't worry. I'll be the one getting nasty with them!' Tom promised grimly. And he turned on his heel and ran, racing madly around the corner after Frank and the sneering youths.

'Give me my money!' demanded Frank, as he

cornered the boys in a narrow sidestreet behind a Chinese restaurant. He tried to stop his knees from shaking. He couldn't let them know he was scared.

'You're boring, kid,' said Skull and Crossbones, advancing towards him menacingly. 'It's our money now.' He turned to the youths behind him. 'Whose money is it?'

'Ours!' they all yelled, laughing like hyenas.

'So rack off!' said Skull and Crossbones.

'No! It's mine!' screamed Frank, demented. He lost all control of his temper and charged at the grotty leader, pummelling him ineffectually with his little fists. The other boys came to Skull and Crossbones' aid, and before Frank knew what was happening, he was kicked and punched to the ground. The next few seconds felt like hours, as his battered senses endured sharp blows on every part of his body, the boys gathered around him like a pack of wild animals, devouring their prey. He writhed in pain on the litter-filled ground, too frightened and shocked to move. He wondered if they were going to kill him, and then – suddenly – he heard a familiar voice. But this time it was raised in fury.

'Leave him alone, you young mongrels!'

And the youths were lifted off him and thrown

aside by strong male arms. Frank dimly gazed up to find Tom – Wimphead! – coming to his rescue. His face was white with anger as he threw the boys off one by one, 'til Skull and Crossbones was the only one left who dared to take him on.

'What's it to you, Grandad?' he jeered.

'I'm his foster father. Why don't you cowards pick on someone your own size?' demanded Tom.

The boy's face reddened. 'No one calls me a coward!' he screamed, lunging at Tom with clenched fists.

Frank was surprised to hear himself crying, 'Leave Tom alone, you scumface!' But he was soon even more surprised to discover that Tom was completely capable of matching Skull and Crossbones. In fact, he pummelled him to the ground in about thirty seconds flat! Frank was amazed to see that Wimphead – *Tom* – was such a good fighter. The other boys ran away in fear of Tom's wrath, and the next thing Frank knew, Pippa knelt beside him, speaking warm words softly and making him feel safe.

'Poor Frank, look at you, darling. What have they done to you? Come on, let's get you home.'

She scooped him up in her arms and carried him

to the car. Tom followed, nursing his own minor bruises. He ruffled Frank's hair gently. 'He'll be right, won't you, mate?'

'Yeah, I'll be right, Tom,' Frank replied faintly. He didn't see the delighted smile that passed between Tom and Pippa. It was the first time he'd addressed either of them by their Christian name. In fact, Frank didn't see much of anything. He was tired and over-excited and sore, and soon he was out like a light . . .

'How's that feel?' Tom asked, prodding Frank's chest gently. It was later that night and Frank was tucked up safe and sound in bed.

'Hurts . . .' sighed the wounded warrior.

'No wonder,' grinned Tom. 'Those blokes gave you quite a going-over.'

Frank smiled up at him. 'You gave them a going-over too,' he said proudly.

'Yeah, I s'pose I did,' smiled Tom. 'But I couldn't see any other way around it. And it doesn't make fighting right.' He paused, then looked Frank deep in the eyes. 'I don't like violence, Frank. I didn't like it when I was a soldier in Vietnam, and I don't like it now.'

Frank's eyes opened wide. 'You fought in Vietnam?!'

Tom nodded.

'Tell me about it!'

'Only if you promise to go to sleep afterwards . . .'

Frank nodded eagerly. 'I promise.'

So for the next half hour Tom told Frank all about his eighteen months spent serving in Vietnam. He described the battles won, the battles lost, the mateship and the loneliness, the fear of death, the laughter. He told Frank about dreaming of home, and sobbing over dead mate's bodies, and rescuing Pippa's brother Danny from a mine. Frank was filled with admiration for the brave man sitting on the end of his bed. He wanted to hear more and more, but Pippa arrived in his bedroom doorway and softly chastised her husband. 'Hey, we've got a boy who needs some sleep in here, darling. I think it's lights out time.'

Tom smiled and raised his hands in mock surrender. 'Fair enough.'

'Will you tell me more tomorrow night?' asked Frank.

'You bet.'

Tom stood up and walked to the door. Pippa came over to Frank's bed and sat down beside him, stroking his hair. He didn't mind this time.

74

She had nice soft hands. He gazed up at her. She was pretty. She didn't really look like like a frog. She kissed him on the forehead and he closed his eyes. 'Good night, Frank.'

'Goodnight.'

' "Night, mate,' said Tom. They walked out, closing the door behind them.

Frank opened his eyes and stared up through the darkness at the ceiling. He felt kind of good – warm and comfy – sort of like he knew Tom and Pippa would never let anything happen to him. Maybe he'd hang around for a while after all? They weren't that bad really. Tom beat Skull and Crossbones to a pulp! And what about those fantastic Vietnam stories? Wow! He sure didn't seem like a wimp anymore. And they hadn't yelled at him for taking their money. In fact, they hadn't said anything about it. Yeah, Tom and Pippa weren't so bad. Maybe he'd give them another chance? But if they turned out to be dags, he'd be off like a shot! He settled back against the pillow and fell into sleep.

Two weeks later Frank was riding his new blue bike in the Fletcher's backyard, when Tom and Pippa came home from shopping, carrying an exciting purchase. 'Look, Frank!' cried Pippa. 'It's one of those new Polaroid cameras. They take instant photos.'

'Wow!' Frank examined the exotic contraption.

'I'm going to go next door and ask Mrs McManus to take a photo of all of us together,' said Tom. 'We haven't got a photo of the whole family yet, have we?'

Frank tried not to smile when Tom said 'family'. He already had a family of his own, but well, with Dad in prison and Mum gone away some-where, he may as well hang out with Tom and Pippa. The last two weeks had been okay. In fact, he kind of liked it here.

Pippa stood on Frank's left side and Tom stood on his right. They both put an arm around his shoulders.

'Smile!' said Mrs McManus. 'Say cheese!'

'Cheese!' Tom, Pippa and Frank beamed into the Polaroid camera. Mrs McManus took three photos, so they could each have one to keep. Then she went back next door to finish hemming her kitchen curtains, and Tom and Pippa went inside. Left alone, sitting on the back step beside his blue bike, Frank took out his photo. They looked like a proper family. The way Pippa was smiling down at him you'd think she really loved him. Well she did. She'd told him. He smiled to himself. And Tom had dark hair like his. Maybe people who saw them together thought he was Tom's real son?

He hoped he'd grow up to be just like Tom. He wanted to be a brave strong soldier who'd save his mates and his country. And he'd marry a girl just like Pippa, a smiley girl with big warm eyes who made everybody feel nice. He liked being in the photo. He liked being with Tom and Pippa. And he realised as he sat perched on the step, that what he wanted most of all was to stay with them for always.

chapter four

The beautiful blonde sat gazing out to sea, her heart filled with a sadness that surprised her with its depth. She'd known this day would arrive eventually, but she hadn't expected it to come so soon. And in spite of everything she'd said and done, she'd always harboured a secret hope that she would be the lucky bride when Frank Morgan married.

But then, she'd had her chance, and she'd blown it. She knew that. But knowing it didn't make the pain any easier to bear, and it certainly didn't stop her loving Frank with all her heart.

'A penny for them Roo.'

Ruth Stewart turned to see her step-mother Ailsa strolling towards her with a smile. 'I was on my way to the liquor store to make sure your Dad closes up in time for the wedding, but there's no big hurry. Want some company for a few minutes?'

Roo nodded wordlessly, and Ailsa slipped down

onto the grassy knoll beside her. As the two women sat together silently, Roo reflected on their changed relationship. Hard to believe she'd once considered Ailsa her enemy. She'd tried every dirty trick in the book to break up Ailsa's marriage to her father, Alf. Roo sighed. She was a different person back then. She'd treated everyone badly – especially Frank. There he was again. Frank . . . Frank . . . if only she could stop thinking about him.

'It's Frank, isn't it?' Ailsa asked shrewdly.

Roo nodded, then sighed. She stared out at the wind-tossed waves, willing herself to feel better. 'I love him Ailsa, I still love him.'

Her voice shook with the tears she longed to cry as Ailsa put a comforting arm around her. She leaned her head against her step-mother's shoulder.

'I thought so, love.' Ailsa stroked her hair. 'This can't be an easy day for you.' They sat in contemplative silence, then Ailsa made a suggestion. 'You don't have to go to the wedding you know. Your dad and I could make an excuse for you.'

Roo sat up straight. She sniffled and wiped her eyes. 'No, I've got to go. I've got to see him marry Bobby so I know for sure there's no hope for me. So I can . . . get on with the rest of my life, you know?'

Ailsa nodded. 'I know.' She paused for a moment. 'Well I think you're a very brave girl.'

Roo shrugged. 'I sure don't feel brave. I feel like I'm falling into a million pieces.' Her chest heaved with misery. 'Why did I do it, Ailsa? He loved me! Why did I lie to him and make him hate me? If I didn't we'd be married now, and we'd have –'

'But you did, Roo,' interrupted Ailsa gently. 'And it's all behind you. Look, I know how much it hurts for you to see Frank marrying Bobby, but what happened between you and Frank happened for a reason. I really believe that. There's somebody else for you, love, somebody every bit as wonderful as Frank. And when you meet him you'll appreciate him twice as much because you've been through all this suffering.'

'Maybe,' shrugged Roo.

'Definitely!' declared Ailsa. 'Now I really should go and hurry your dad up. If being late was a sport he'd be captain of the Olympic team!'

Roo smiled as her stepmother climbed to her feet. 'Thanks, Ailsa.'

'No worries, kiddo,' Ailsa grinned. 'That was a free consultation. See you at home in a few minutes?'

80

Roo nodded. Ailsa gave her one final pat on the shoulder, and headed off to hurry her husband.

Roo turned her attention back to the ocean. She thought of the times she and Frank had clowned around on the edge of the water, with the sound of waves and the fresh, salty smell of the sea all around them. She wished with all her heart she could bring those days back, but she knew she never could. She shouldn't even yearn for them, because the past was the past, and Frank belonged to Bobby now. She smiled sadly at a seagull that fluttered nearby in the vain hope of breadcrumbs.

It was good of Ailsa to try and console her, but Roo didn't believe she'd find somebody else. Not someone like Frank. At the moment all she could think of was how she'd ruined her own life by nearly ruining his. Poor Frank. He was so gentle, so caring, so easily hurt. Roo sighed. She hadn't been the first girl to cause him pain. She remembered the tales Frank had told her about his first romances. It seemed his lovelife had never been smooth!

Frank strode self-consciously across the playground. He felt as though he was on display. His arms swung awkwardly by his sides, and the tarred quadrangle seemed to get wider with every step. He hated school. He felt eyes burning into his back and wondered why he always seemed to attract such stares. He supposed it was because the kids had somehow heard about his father. But he was wrong.

The other students stared because fifteen-year-old Frank Morgan was quite extraordinarily good-looking. His deep brown eyes were fringed by long lashes, his hair was black and silky smooth, and he had a physique most teenage boys only dreamed about possessing. Many of the girls secretly thought he looked just like the swarthy heroes in the romance novels they regularly devoured.

Frank, loping across the playground towards his trio of mates, was completely unaware of his physical attraction. But the same certainly couldn't be said for Melissa Fitzpatrick and her vicious friend Emily Green, who watched him from beneath a nearby tree, with hungry eyes.

Melissa Fitzpatrick was the most popular girl in Year Ten. She had long blonde hair, big blue eyes and a natural tan that seemed to last all year. Her father was a prominent barrister and she lived in the poshest part of the city. Melissa was pretty, brainy and fun, and the top player in the Year Ten netball team. The girls envied her, while the boys vied hopelessly for her attention – hopelessly because they knew she was going steady with Ashley Kieran.

Melissa had been going out with seventeen-year-old Ashley Kieran for over three months. She was the only girl in Year Ten who had a boyfriend in Year Twelve. And Ashley Kieran certainly wasn't just any old boyfriend! He was School Captain – tall, handsome and the best right winger the senior rugby league team had ever possessed. Everyone said he and Melissa made the perfect couple. So even though other boys tried to crack onto her, they knew it was a lost cause. Melissa only had eyes for Ashley.

And that's what Melissa had thought too – until she'd found herself staring at Frank Morgan in the classroom, across the playground, trying to get him to notice her; not knowing what it was that made her want to sit beside him, get to know him, feel his arms around her, kiss those Mediterranean-looking lips . . .

She shivered to herself, hoping Emily hadn't noticed. What was wrong with her? Frank Morgan was definitely not her type! He didn't even have a proper family. He was fostered out to that wimpy Fletcher lady who came on tuck-shop duty sometimes. The clothes she wore were so dull and sensible – the woman had no idea!

And Melissa had heard a rumour that Frank's real father was in gaol. For drugs! God, why was she even looking at him? It was a question she couldn't answer. He wasn't in the top class for any subject. Actually, he was a bit of a dumbo from the sound of things. He spent all his time hanging out with three daggy jerks from the D classes. They'd formed some rock and roll band, apparently. He didn't excel on the sports field either, not like Ashley.

She watched him as he met up with his friends. They said something that made him turn and stare across the playground at her! She felt her face burning as she turned hurriedly away. Those eyes! They really did something to her! She couldn't help it – the way they slid in her direction sometimes was just so sexy. And his face – it looked like God had decided to mould the perfect male features. She could tell he'd be the passionate type. So –

'What are you staring at that jerk Frank Morgan for?'

Melissa jumped guiltily as Emily interrupted her dreamy train of thought. 'I wasn't,' she lied.

'Well you wouldn't want to,' Emily said nastily. 'He's a total nobody. His father's in gaol, they reckon.'

'I know that,' said Melissa. Emily's observation made her feel uncomfortable. 'I'm going to go find Ashley.' And she strolled away, self-consciously casual.

84

Left alone, Emily's gaze burned in Frank's direction, her eyes narrowed with hatred. How dare he say no when she'd asked him out last week? He should be so lucky that a pretty, popular girl like Emily would pay any attention to him in the first place! Melissa and the others didn't know about it of course. She hadn't told them. But Frank Morgan would live to regret the day he knocked back Emily Green! She bit her lip anxiously. And now it looked as though Melissa was interested. Emily couldn't let that happen. If Melissa asked him out, he'd say yes for sure. Boys always did with Melissa. And if Emily couldn't have him, no-one would! So watch out, stupid Frank Morgan, Emily Green's out to ruin your life!

'I tell ya, mate. She's got the hots for ya!'

Across the other side of the playground, Frank's mate Stephen (Stud) Clarke was ribbing him about Melissa. 'Could see it in her eyes, Morgan. You're in!'

Frank couldn't believe that a girl as popular and pretty as Melissa Fitzpatrick would be the vaguest bit interested. But his mates seemed convinced.

'He's right, Morgo,' said James (Jimbo) Duggan. 'She can't take her eyes off ya!'

'Quick! Turn around and check it out!' urged Geoff (Peabrain) Purvis. 'Go on!'

Frank gingerly turned his head in Melissa's direction, amazed to instantly meet her gaze. He turned away, embarrassed.

'Told ya!' Stud poked him in the ribs. 'What I want to know is, but, why's she perving on you when you're standing next to a sex machine like me?'

Frank grinned. Stud was only half joking. He'd earned his nickname from an early age. At only fifteen, he was already going out with girls as old as seventeen and eighteen! He was a brawny, good-looking blond who exuded heaps of natural charm. Stud was a consistent non-performer in the classroom, but what he lacked in scholastic success, he more than made up for in confidence. He was thrilled when selected drummer with Frank's new group, The Remedial Class. After all, everyone knew that girls went crazy over guys in bands!

The remainder of The Remedial Class consisted of Frank on lead guitar and vocals, James (Jimbo) Duggan on bass guitar, and Geoff (Peabrain) Purvis on keyboards. Stud, Jimbo and Peabrain were Frank's best mates. They were a bedraggled bunch, drawn together by their academic apathy and love of music.

Jimbo was a five foot five dynamo, a plump guy with a bouncy personality who brightened up any room he entered. If things got a bit aggro at band rehearsals, Jimbo could always be relied upon to crack a joke and relieve the tension. His happy-go-lucky outlook was infectious. Everyone loved Jimbo.

Peabrain was a huge, hulking teenager who looked like the Incredible Hulk but had the personality of a kitten. Peabrain was gentle, calm and kind. He occasionally reminded Frank of his childhood friend, the tranquil Sam Green. Although ungifted intellectually, Peabrain possessed a rare talent on keyboards. The other guys considered themselves lucky to have him as an integral member of The Remedial Class.

'What are ya going to do about it, Morgan?' asked Stud.

'She wants ya to ask her out, I bet,' surmised Jimbo.

Frank blushed scarlet. 'Hah, she doesn't. Look, she's walking away.'

'That's only 'cause you caught her pervin,' Stud assured him. 'She's dyin' for ya, Morgan! I can tell.'

Frank hardly dared believe it could be true. He'd often thought Melissa Fitzpatrick was cute, but it had never occurred to him in his wildest dreams that the feeling might be mutual! 'Ya reckon?'

'Yeah, I reckon, Moron Morgan!' ribbed Stud good-naturedly. He gave Frank a pretend punch in the stomach.

'Ask her out, mate,' urged Peabrain.

'You'd have to be a screw loose not to!' enthused Jimbo. 'She's a real spunk!'

The other boys nodded their heads in enthusiastic agreement.

'Do you reckon she's keen on me?' Frank asked Peabrain. He knew Peabrain wouldn't lie.

'Yeah, mate, I do. Honest.'

Frank still thought it was too good to be true. 'But she goes out with that Kieran guy.'

'So?' sighed Stud, a man of the world. 'She's obviously not gettin' what she wants outa him, if the way she was checkin' you out's got anything to do with it!'

'Maybe,' Frank pondered uncertainly. 'But why would she be interested in me?'

Stud grinned. 'Because you're a cool, good-lookin' guy who's startin' a band that's gonna go straight to the top, that's why, Moron!'

Frank laughed. Maybe Stud was right? 'Yeah.'
He paused. 'So what do I do?'

'You ask her out!!!' Stud exclaimed impatiently.
'How many times do we have to tell ya? Not
chicken are ya?'

'Course not!' Frank lied.

'Good,' said Stud. ''Cause if you didn't ask her,
we'd be forced to think you were too gutless,
wouldn't we, fellas?'

'Yeah,' grinned Jimbo.

'Yeah we would,' smirked Peabrain.

'And what kind of professional muso is a
chicken?' taunted Stud.

Frank gulped. 'All right. I get the message. I'll
ask her to the gig on Friday night.'

'Good on ya, mate! You'll be laughin'!'

And the lesson bell rang.

Later that afternoon in class, as the boring teacher Mrs Pead droned on about the Peruvian
rainfall, Frank felt his mind wandering back to
what the fellas had said earlier. He sighed. He'd
have to ask her out, or they'd think he was
gutless. He carved the initials MF in his old
wooden desk. Maybe they'd imagined the whole
thing? Maybe she wasn't interested? Maybe she'd
been looking at someone behind him?

But even as he asked himself these questions, Frank knew the answers. She was interested. He'd seen it in her eyes. It wasn't the first time he'd caught her looking, either. But the other times he'd decided he must have been imagining things. But his mates wouldn't imagine it too. It must be true! He felt a little thrill of delight, then a sudden rush of terror. He hoped he'd be able to talk to her alone, away from the mousey-haired Emily Green. He knew Emily'd had it in for him ever since he'd said no thanks when she'd asked him to that barbeque. And what if Melissa said no? What if she laughed in his face and spread it around the playground? Well, he reasoned, he'd have to take that chance. After all, he had nothing to lose.

Frank hated school. He loathed almost everything about it. From the headmaster, Mr Drummond, who picked on him incessantly, to the brainy kids, who considered themselves so superior to the likes of Frank; and the athletic ones who judged everybody by how high they could jump, or how fast they could run. They all wrote Frank off as a dead loss. He knew it. They whispered about his father's record, and speculated on whether he'd turn out the same. The teachers pressured him relentlessly to improve his performance in the classroom. But the only performance Frank wanted to improve was that of The Remedial Class.

As soon as Year Ten was over he planned to leave this putrid place and put all his efforts into managing the band. He knew Tom and Pippa weren't thrilled about this state of affairs, but well, basically that was tough luck. Apart from his foster parents, the band members were the only people who made him feel he was needed. His friendship with the guys was what kept him going. Stud, Peabrain and Jimbo were his only reason for coming to school ... until Melissa.

Melissa perched daintily on the edge of her school-case. She knew she was the best-looking girl at the bus stop, especially sitting like this. Her uniform rode up high when she crossed her shapely knees. Not too high, but just high enough. Boys commented on her tanned legs as they passed by. She pretended not to notice, but she did, of course. Usually it didn't matter, because Ashley was with her, but he was staying back to study today. Melissa was glad. It left her time to daydream.

She buried her pretty blonde head in one of the Year Ten English novels, letting her thoughts drift back to Frank Morgan. Those smouldering eyes ... that incredible face ... the way he'd looked at her today had almost made her knees melt! She knew he was interested in her too. And she also knew he walked home this way ...

and, gulp, look relaxed, Melissa . . . there he was now, turning the corner!

There she was, sitting on her schoolcase. God, she looked fantastic. Check the legs! he thought to himself. He was relieved to note that she was alone. No sign of Ashley, or the dreaded Emily Green. Great. That'd make it easier. He took a deep breath. What if she said no? Or worse, what if she laughed at him?

Wow, look at the way he walks. He's so cool and confident, she told herself. So in control of the situation. He's getting closer. What would she say when he asked her out? How would she stop herself from blushing? Then a horrible thought occurred. What if he didn't ask her out? What if he just sauntered past?

He swallowed nervously, his heart in his mouth.

She flicked her hair over her shoulder shyly.

She was gorgeous . . .

He was so sexy . . .

He was getting closer to the girl on the school-case . . .

He's only ten feet away!

Here goes . . . 'Hi'

He spoke to me! 'Hello.'

92

Frank heaved an inward sigh of relief. At least she wasn't going to ignore him. 'How are ya going?'

'Good thanks.'

Melissa tried not to blush. Frank Morgan was so together. What if he thought she was a tongue-tied kid?

Frank tried to look casual. So far so good. In for a penny, in for a pound. He took a breath and bit the bullet. 'Ah, are you doing anything on Friday night?'

Melissa relaxed. He liked her. Thank Goodness. She favoured him with her most seductive smile. 'No, nothing special. Why?'

Looks like she might say yes! Here goes ... 'My band's playing at the town hall dance. Would you like to come with me?'

Melissa tried to hide her excitement under a casual air. 'Yeah, I'd love to.'

Wow! She'd said yes! He couldn't believe it! He was over-the-moon! But he couldn't let her see that. She'd think he was a dag. 'Great. I'll talk to you about it at school tomorrow, okay?'

'Okay.'

'See you later.'

chapter four

'Bye.'

Frank sauntered away slowly, struggling against the overwhelming temptation to run down the street like a madman. Melissa was coming to see the band! He could hardly believe it. Hey, Frank, calm down, be cool . . . he waited until he had turned the corner to jump in the air and yell a loud 'Yipee!'

Melissa watched Frank disappear around the corner, her face alight with a glorious grin. He was so cool, so casual, so . . . and those eyes! Would she ever be able to look into them without feeling that she might die? She was going to see his band on Friday night! What would she wear? Where would she sit? Would he dedicate a song to her? Would he walk her home later? What would it be like to kiss those luscious lips?

'Why are you looking so pleased with yourself?' Emily plonked her schoolcase down and sat herself beside her best friend. Melissa gave her a secretive smile. 'Promise you won't tell Ashley?'

'Of course I promise.'

Melissa leaned forward and lowered her voice. She smiled almost apologetically. 'Well, I know you'll think I'm stupid,' she began defensively, 'but Frank Morgan just asked me out and I said yes!'

Emily's face hardened. This was exactly what she had dreaded! If Frank Morgan wouldn't go out with her, he certainly wasn't going out with any of her friends! What if he told Melissa that she, Emily, had tried to crack onto him? Melissa would tell everyone else. She'd die! Well, Emily wouldn't let that happen. If she couldn't be happy, as far as she was concerned, no one should be. Especially not Frank Morgan! Stuff that guy! He always ruined everything!

'You're mad!' she screamed at her friend. 'He's a total derro! He probably can't even spell his own name – that's if he knows what it is. He doesn't even live with his real parents.'

Melissa stood her ground. 'I know all that, but I can't help it. I'm always looking at him and thinking about kissing him and stuff.'

'Well you'll just have to stop thinking about kissing the jerk!' insisted the vindictive Emily. 'He's in all the dumb classes, he hangs around with a pack of dags, he's got no money, and he doesn't even play football!'

Melissa felt herself wilting under Emily's disapproval. She bit her lip anxiously. Emily moved in for the kill. 'You go out with the most gorgeous guy in the whole school, Melissa. Think about it. What do you want that Ashley hasn't got?'

Melissa was silent. She couldn't think of anything. Emily pounced triumphantly. 'See? There's nothing, is there? Every other girl in the school would kill to go out with Ashley, and you're going to risk losing all that for a deadhead like Frank Morgan? You must be out of your tree!'

Melissa felt her resolve weakening. Maybe Emily had a point?

'Face it, Melissa. Frank's a loser. And the fact is, if you start going out with him, everyone's going to think you're a loser too.'

Emily knew the last thing Melissa would ever want was other kids thinking she was a loser. She felt sure she could rest her case. She was right.

'But what can I do?' Melissa asked anxiously. 'I can't stop thinking about him.'

'You have to stop!' Emily urged nastily. 'Otherwise that no-hoper will drag you down with him, and no-one will want to know you!'

Melissa was frantic. 'But how can I stop?!'

'I'll think of something,' promised Emily. 'Don't worry.'

'Okay,' agreed Melissa. She was sorry to be missing out on her date with the gorgeous Frank, but she had to admit that Emily was right.

'I'll work out a good plan, and I'll ring you tonight.'

'Thanks,' said Melissa. She sighed. It would have to be a very good plan, because no matter how hard she tried, she couldn't get those dark brown eyes out of her restless mind!

A couple of hours later at the Fletcher house, Frank put down his knife and fork and wiped his mouth with relish. 'That was delicious, Pippa!'

Pippa and Tom exchanged a smile. Frank was certainly in high spirits tonight.

'Glad it meets with your approval, sir,' grinned Pippa.

'Can I be excused please?' asked Frank. 'I want to go upstairs and practise my guitar.'

'Sure thing, mate,' said Tom. 'We'll leave the dishes for you when you're ready.'

Frank stood up, pushing his chair against the table. He grinned lightheartedly. 'Don't panic. It'll get done.' He started walking towards the stairs. 'Catch you later.'

'Catch you later,' said Pippa to his disappearing back. She cleared the dirty dishes from the table. 'He's chirpy,' she observed to her husband.

'Yeah,' agreed Tom. 'Good to see, isn't it? Seems like he enjoyed his day at school for once.'

'Mmmm.' Pippa retreated to the kitchen with the dishes, then returned. She smiled at her husband mischievously. 'Are you thinking what I'm thinking?'

'That tonight might be a good time to raise the subject of Frank staying on at school to do his HSC?'

Pippa nodded. 'You're psychic.'

Tom shrugged. 'Well, it couldn't hurt I s'pose. He's certainly in a more approachable mood than usual.'

'Get in while the going's good,' urged Pippa. 'I'll take care of the dishes.'

'Fair enough.' Tom pushed his chair back from the table and headed up the hallway stairs. At the top of the landing his ears were met by a curious sound. The sound of silence! Where was the ever-present guitar that twanged in Frank's room at all hours? Tom knocked on his foster son's door. 'Can I talk to you for a sec, mate?'

'Sure, Tom, come in.'

Tom opened the door and did a double-take to see Frank seated at his study desk, with his history text books opened in front of him. 'What's all this about? Thought you wanted to do some guitar practice?'

Frank shrugged. 'It's no big deal. Just decided to do some studying instead.'

Tom tried to hide his surprise. This was certainly uncharacteristic behaviour! 'Well, good on you.'

Frank looked at him curiously. 'Spit it out, Tom. What do you want to talk to me about?'

Tom sank down onto Frank's bed. He sighed and clasped his hands together awkwardly. 'Well, mate, it's like this. I know you and the blokes are having a great time setting up this band, the Slow Learners –'

'That's The Remedial Class, Tom,' Frank grinned.

'Oh yeah, sorry,' Tom smiled sheepishly. 'But what Pippa and I are concerned about, is that –'

'If I leave school after Year 10 and devote all my time to the band, I won't have a solid education behind me to find a real job if I ever need one. Right?' Frank finished for him.

'Yeah, right,' Tom agreed, relieved to be met halfway. 'That's it in a nutshell, I guess.'

'Well you don't have to worry,' said Frank. 'I've been thinking about it, and I've decided it's time I got my act together with my school work.'

'You have?' Tom was amazed.

'Yeah I have,' Frank assured his foster father. He

leaned forward confidentially, beaming from ear to ear. 'You know what happened today? I asked this incredible girl called Melissa out, and she said yes!'

'Well you've never had a high knock-back rate.'

'I know that,' said Frank patiently, 'but Melissa's different. She's got everything Tom. Beautiful blonde hair, big blue eyes, great body, brains, the lot. Every guy in the school wants to go out with her, and she said yes to me!'

'Well good for you, mate,' smiled Tom.

'I always thought I was a loser. I didn't even believe the guys when they said she liked me, but they were right. And girls like that don't hang around with losers, Tom. So I'm going to work my guts out and really try and get somewhere with my schoolwork. I can still run the band. It just needs a bit of organisation.'

Tom patted him on the shoulder, delighted. 'Well I'm impressed. I came up here to deliver a pep talk, but I can't find anyone who needs one, so I guess I'll leave you to it.'

'Sure. See you.'

Tom walked out, closing the door behind him. Pippa was waiting at the bottom of the stairs. 'That was quick. A pointless exercise was it?'

'Far from it,' beamed Tom. 'He's decided to — quote — "work his guts out" with his school-work.'

Pippa smiled delightedly. 'That's great!' She pulled a puzzled face. 'But why the sudden turn-around?'

'I believe they call it love,' said Tom drily. 'And all I can say is, thank God for Melissa Whats-her-name!'

On the other side of the city, Emily waited impatiently for the Fitzpatrick 'phone to be answered. She knew Melissa's house was large, but this was ridiculous. It couldn't take them a full five minutes to walk to the nearest telephone! Emily's nerves were on edge. She'd thought of a foolproof plan to make sure Melissa and Frank never got to know each other properly, but she'd let Melissa do the dirty work for her. Emily would have the pleasure of seeing Pretty Boy Morgan's face rubbed in the dirt. That'd show him — the stupid little derro! He should have jumped at the chance of going out with Emily. Well, boy oh boy, was he ever going to regret the day he'd said no! And the best part was, he'd blame Melissa. And he'd never want to see her again!

'Hullo?' A pretty feminine voice answered on the other end of the phone.

chapter four

'About time, Melissa!' snapped Emily. 'I haven't got all night!'

'Oh, hi Emily,' said Melissa. 'Have you thought of something?'

'I certainly have,' gloated Emily gleefully. 'Look, the only way to get this jerk out of your system is to make sure he gets you out of his. And that means being cruel to be kind. Okay?'

'Okay, I guess . . .' mumbled Melissa uncertainly.

'Get your act together, girl!' snarled Emily. 'Do you want everyone to start treating you like you've got leprosy?'

'Of course not!'

'Well that's what they'll do if you go out with Frank Morgan.'

'All right,' acknowledged Melissa. 'So what's the plan?'

'You've got to make sure he never wants to look at you again,' instructed Emily. 'You've got to rub his face in the dirt and then kick him while he's down. And I know the perfect way to do it.'

'How?'

Emily smiled maliciously. 'I thought you'd never ask!'

chapter five

Steven Matheson tightened his bow-tie and turned around in front of the mirror. He grinned at his foster brother Frank. 'Check me out. I'm beautiful!'

Frank hit him over the head with a bath towel. 'Get real, Stevo,' he smiled. 'I'm the groom, remember?'

'A minor detail, Frank,' said Steven, as he combed his hair carefully, flicking a speck of dandruff from his collar. Frank rolled his eyes good-naturedly. 'Do you think I could get near the mirror for a second?'

'Sorry, Frank. Possession's nine-tenths of the law.'

'Yeah? Well I make the laws around here! This is my place. Remember?' Frank playfully pushed his foster brother out of the way.

'Hey! Careful of the merchandise!' grinned Steven, shoving Frank back with more force than he realised.

'Watch it!' Frank stumbled and felt himself falling. His flailing arms grabbed Steven and dragged him down too.

'Careful!'

They fell in a heap on the bathroom floor, laughing. "'Struth! The tuxes!" groaned Frank, climbing clumsily to his feet. 'The groom can't arrive at the church in a crumpled suit.' He brushed himself off. 'Neither can the best man.'

Steven smiled cockily. 'Best man. I like the sound of that.'

'Don't know why you were surprised I asked you,' said Frank. 'You're my best mate aren't you?'

Steven grinned delightedly. 'Yeah, s'pose I am.' He paused. 'I sure wasn't for a while though. Remember when I first came to live with Tom and Pippa? You hated my guts!'

'That was only 'cause I had it in for brainy kids,' explained Frank, tying his bow tie carefully.

'Yeah, I know,' remembered Steven. 'How come?'

Frank shrugged. 'I was sick of being hassled by 'em.'

Steven checked that his fingernails were clean.

He turned to his foster brother, head on one side. 'I always knew some your teachers gave you a hard time. Tom and Pippa told me. But something else happened didn't it? Some kids tried to wreck things for you or something?'

Frank combed his hair carefully. He didn't like talking about this stuff much. It brought the memories back all too clearly. 'Yeah, they did.'

'What happened?' asked Steven. 'You've never said.' When Frank remained silent, he pressed the question. 'You can tell your best man can't you?'

Frank thought for a moment. Then he shrugged his shoulders. Why not? The Emily Greens, Melissa Fitzpatricks and Ashley Kierans of the world didn't matter anymore. What did he care about jerks like them? He was about to marry the most fantastic girl any guy had ever met, he had a job he loved with the Micklin Corporation, and he was surrounded by caring friends. He stuck a rose in his black lapel. 'Well, Steve, it was like this . . .'

The Remedial Class finished the number with a flourish.

'And I find myself consumed with fear
When I find you standing near . . . oh yeah!'

It was an original song Frank had written a couple of months before. The guys were really proud of the way they had it mastered. They crowded around, patting one another on the back, congratulating themselves on their prowess.

'There's only, one word for us – brilliant!' enthused Stephen (Stud) Clarke.

'We did that number really great,' agreed Pea-brain.

'Top song, Morgan!' Jimbo congratulated Frank.

'Yeah, but this is only a rehearsal in a garage,' Frank reminded his musical mates. 'Friday night's the big test – the gig at the town hall dance.'

The other guys refused to be sobered.

'We'll laugh it in!' enthused Stud.

'We're goin' to be the biggest thing since INXS!' declared Jimbo.

'All that money, all those women!' raved Stud. 'I can hardly wait!'

'Well we'd better not count our chickens before they're hatched,' warned Frank.

'Get real, Morgan!' Stud remonstrated. 'Stop being on such a downer. In a few months we'll all be finished with cruddy school and we can spend all our time rehearsing. It'll be a one way trip to the top, mate.'

106

Frank felt instantly guilty. He hadn't told the guys about his change of plans yet. He knew they wouldn't like it, but well, that was tough. Now was as good a time as any. 'Look, I've been thinking about that, and I reckon I'll probably stay on at school and try and make a go of it with my lessons and stuff.'

His three friends stared at him in stunned disbelief.

'It doesn't mean I'll be dumping the band. I can still spend all my spare time practising. I'll manage both. It'll be okay.

An angry Stud broke the startled silence. 'Have you gone mental?!' he demanded. 'You were the one who said we should go full-time with the band in the first place!'

'I know,' admitted Frank, embarrassed, 'but I don't know, when Melissa said she'd come to the dance with me, it got me thinking and –'

'What?!' yelled Stud. 'You've decided to stay at school with a pack of stuck-up creeps, just because that snobby chick said she'd go out with you?! You've gone mental!'

'She's not snobby!' Frank retorted.

'She is, mate,' said Jimbo. 'She's as snobby as they come.'

'They're right, Morgan,' agreed the gentle Peabrain. 'She thinks she's better than everybody else.'

Frank stared at the rest of The Remedial Class, amazed. 'What are you on about? You're the ones who told me to ask her out!'

'Yeah, but we didn't tell you to suddenly decide you're too good for the band!' declared Stud. 'You've never put chicks before The Remedial Class before, Morgan. What's happening to you?'

'You hate school as much as the rest of us,' Jimbo asserted. 'What do you want to put yourself through another two years of it for?'

'I know what for!' scoffed Stud. 'So he can be near Miss High and Mighty Melissa and all her stuck-up buddies.'

Frank refused to take the bait. He was determined not to let his mates sway him from his new objective. 'Look, I'm sorry if it doesn't suit you guys, but I'm staying on, and that's all there is to it.' He avoided meeting their accusing eyes. 'Now I reckon we should rehearse another number.' He returned his guitar.

Frank failed to realize the depth of the band members' disappointment. Twenty-four hours later Stud, Jimbo and Peabrain held a secret meeting at Stud's place to discuss the group's uncertain future. Stud said decisions had to be made.

'I feel like a bit of a scum not asking Morgan over too,' said Jimbo guiltily.

'Me too,' agreed Peabrain.

Stud rolled his eyes in disgust. 'We couldn't invite him, 'cause he's what we've got to talk about.'

'Yeah, I s'pose,' Jimbo acknowledged half-heartedly.

Peabrain and Jimbo sunk into a couple of bean bags on Stud's loungeroom floor. His parents were out so they wouldn't be hassled. Stud leaned on the edge of a table. He stared at his mates purposefully. 'Well . . .'

'I wish we'd never talked him into asking Melissa Fitzpatrick out,' sighed Peabrain regretfully.

'Yeah,' agreed Jimbo. 'I mean she's good-looking, that's for sure, but she's *really up herself*.'

'And she'll change Morgan,' Stud predicted ominously. 'Wait and see. They haven't even had their first date and he's already decided that school's more important than The Remedial Class.'

'He didn't say that,' Jimbo pointed out.

'No, but that's what he meant,' declared Stud. 'Think about it. If he stays at school he'll have assignments and tests and stuff. He won't have time to chase gigs as well. He'll start not turning up to rehearsals, then we'll have to cancel gigs at the last minute 'cause he can't show.'

Jimbo and Peabrain exchanged a worried glance. They didn't like Frank being criticized, but they had to admit that Stud had a point.

'What we've got to do to make it work,' asserted Stud, 'is get jobs we don't care about, where we can *chuck sickies* when we want to for rehearsals, and pack it in when the band starts taking off.'

Jimbo and Peabrain nodded in agreement. Stud could see they were coming round to his way of thinking. He pressed the point. 'What's the number one priority?' Stud challenged them.

'The band,' they both replied instantly.

'Right!' enthused Stud. 'And can we afford to have a band member who doesn't feel that way?'

Jimbo was shocked. 'We can't kick Morgan out of the band!'

'We might have to,' Stud raised his hands regretfully. 'Look, I like him as much as you blokes do.

110

He's a good mate. But if the band's going to come first every member has to have the right attitude.' He paused to let his point sink in. 'Am I right?'

Jimbo and Peabrain nodded halfheartedly. 'Yeah.' They were silent for a moment, then the loyal Jimbo made a suggestion. 'But let's see how it goes, eh? We don't have to do anything yet. Maybe we can get him to change his mind about school?'

'Yeah, that's what we've gotta do,' agreed the gentle Peabrain.

Stud nodded, frowning. 'But to change his mind about school we've got to change his mind about Melissa.'

And even Frank's three worried friends didn't realise how hard that would be! Frank was well and truly smitten with the pretty Melissa Fitz-patrick.

As he dressed for the dance on Friday night, unaware of the band's secret plans, Frank found his mind fully occupied with thoughts of the beautiful blonde. He still couldn't believe his luck. He smiled suavely at the bathroom mirror as he liberally splashed Tom's best aftershave all over his face and neck.

'Hey, I saw that!' Tom appeared, grinning, in

the narrow doorway. 'That's my best stuff, mate. Hope you're going to replace it.'

'Sure thing, Tom,' smiled Frank, tongue-in-cheek. 'I'll buy you a new bottle when I make my first million.'

Tom leaned against the door frame. He smiled with gruff affection at his foster son. 'So, tonight's the big night eh? Your most important concert so far.'

'That's gig, Tom.'

'Oh, right . . . so, feeling confident?'

'About the band? Yeah. We'll knock 'em dead.'

'You sound pretty relaxed for someone who looks so nervous.'

The butterflies in Frank's stomach jumped as though Tom had addressed them all personally. 'It's not the band that's worrying me.'

Tom smiled wisely. 'Oh. Melissa whats-her-name, eh?'

'Melissa Fitzpatrick, Tom. And I still can't believe she's coming with me.' He gazed into the mirror rapturously. 'You should see her.'

'S'pose I will a bit later,' Tom smirked. 'You two kids will be wanting a lift, won't you?'

He ducked as Frank threw a bath sponge in his direction.

'Thanks for the thought, but we'll get there ourselves.' Frank pulled a 'ha ha very funny' face at his foster father. 'In fact, s'pose I should get going now, or I'll be late to pick her up.'

'Fair enough,' said Tom. He chuckled. 'Have you got a hanky in case your nose gets runny?'

Frank laughed as he reached for a deadly missile just above the bathtub. Tom artfully dodged the flying face flannel.

An hour later, in the most exclusive part of the city, Melissa Fitzpatrick stole a glance through her pink silk bedroom curtains. She drew them closed hurriedly, moving from the window. 'Here he is, Em! I can see him coming!'

Emily's lips set in a thin line. 'Good. Well you know what to do.'

Melissa sank down on to her four poster bed, tugging at a lock of hair anxiously. 'I don't know, maybe I shouldn't?'

Emily advanced towards her, surprising even Melissa with her vehemence. 'What are you talking about?! You have to, you idiot. Otherwise he'll ruin your life! Everyone'll treat you like dirt for going out with a derro like him!'

'But he's so good-looking . . .'

Emily was all too aware of that fact. And it made her hate Frank Morgan even more. 'So was Tarzan! But do you want to go out with him?'

'No . . .' Melissa said uncertainly.

'You've got to do it Melissa! You've got to!'

Melissa bit her lip, fiddling with a satin ribbon on one of her lace covered cushions. She suddenly looked at her friend suspiciously. 'Why are you so anxious for me to do it? What's it to you?'

Emily felt a cold rush of fear. What if Melissa guessed that she'd once tried to crack on to Frank? She couldn't let that happen! She tried to answer confidently. 'You're my best friend, that's what. And I don't want to see you ruin your life.'

Melissa smiled at Emily guiltily. How could she have thought otherwise? She felt awful for doubting her loyal friend's motives. 'I'm sorry, Em. Of course you're right. I've got to do it. I just don't like it, that's all.'

'Neither do I,' lied Emily, 'but it's the only way.'

The melodic tones of the front doorbell rang throughout the house. Upstairs, Melissa and Emily exchanged a conspiratorial smile.

'You're on!' whispered Emily gleefully. 'Good luck!'

Frank stood on the huge front step, nervously adjusting his collar as he waited for the door to be answered. What a posh house! He'd never known anyone who lived in a place like it. So huge and classy-looking, with a beautiful garden full of trees, and a driveway practically as long as his street. It looked like it came straight from the pages of one of Pippa's home and garden magazines! He felt nervous and inadequate, but he was determined not to show it.

Suddenly Melissa opened the door. His breath caught in his throat. She wore a close-fitting black strapless dress and high-heeled black shoes. Her hair was shining in the moonlight, falling around her shoulders like a golden halo. She looked so gorgeous he could hardly speak.

'Hello, Frank.'

'Hi.'

'Come in.'

'Thanks.'

As Melissa led Frank into the large entrance foyer she tried to still the loud beating of her heart. She felt sure he must be able to hear it! He was so cool, so laid-back. Nothing ever seemed to phase him. And those eyes ... She took a deep breath, then hardened her resolve. No matter how handsome he was, Emily was right. Frank Morgan was a loser and he'd drag her down with him if she allowed him to. She had no choice but to go ahead with the plan. 'Come into the loungeroom and meet my Mum and Dad.'

'Yeah, sure.'

Frank tried not to gape at the expensive antiques and original paintings that filled the spacious hallway. Be casual Frank, be cool ...

She could see him stealing wide-eyed glances at Mum and Dad's collector items. Now was the ideal time to get the ball rolling. 'Like the furniture and stuff do you?'

He smiled. 'Yeah.'

'Don't suppose you've ever seen anything like it before, with your background,' she said deliberately, as she opened a door and led him into the massive loungeroom.

Frank felt instantly uncomfortable. Was he that obvious?

Melissa led him towards an expensively-dressed couple who chatted on the other side of the room. 'Mum, Dad, this is Frank Morgan.'

116

Melissa's affluent-looking parents were reclining on antique chairs, sipping on a pre-dinner drink. Mr Fitzpatrick was tall, broad and commanding, Mrs Fitzpatrick a cool blonde who reeked of elegance. Frank felt immediately intimidated as they looked him up and down judgementally. He was sure his shirt must be crumpled, or his hair all out of place, or something. Mr Fitzpatrick got up from his chair and greeted him with a half-hearted handshake.

'Hullo there Frank.'

'Hullo Mr Fitzpatrick, Mrs Fitzpatrick.'

There was a short silence as they stared at him, sizing him up. Frank felt increasingly awkward. Why didn't Melissa say something to break the ice? Still no-one spoke. Frank felt like he was on display in a department store widow. The seconds seemed like hours.

'Would we know your family, Frank?' asked Mrs Fitzpatrick, eventually.

'Oh, no, Mum,' replied Melissa, laughing. 'You wouldn't know them. Frank hasn't got a proper family.'

Mrs Fitzpatrick frowned. 'Whatever do you mean, dear?'

'Well, he has, but his father's in gaol so he

doesn't live with them.' Melissa turned to Frank, all-innocence. 'It's drugs he's in for, isn't it?'

Mr and Mrs Fitzpatrick went white with shock. Frank prayed for the earth to open up and swallow him. Unfortunately it didn't co-operate. What the hell was Melissa doing? There was another awkward silence, then Mr Fitzpatrick cleared his throat. 'So, in Lissy's class are you Frank?'

'No way, Dad,' said Melissa breezily, before Frank had a chance to reply. 'He's in the lower classes for everything. He's no good at school, but he wants to leave and be in a rock and roll band soon, so it doesn't really matter.'

'I see,' said Mr Fitzpatrick coldly. He exchanged a disapproving glance with his wife. Frank could see the contempt in their eyes. He wished he was like Ashley Kieran. Every parent's dream come true. But he wasn't. He was Frank Morgan, undesirable criminal's son in the lower classes. He hoped Melissa would say something to alleviate the tension, but what she said next only made thngs worse.

'Frank's had a really interesting life, Dad. He came to live with his foster parents because he tried to rob a bank. The police took him into custody.'

118

Listening with her ear pressed against the loungeroom door, Emily smirked with malicious glee
in the hallway. That'd show the stupid derro!
Served him right! She hoped he was squirming.

And he was.

'Well, I suppose we'd better get going,' said
Melissa, after what seemed an eternity.

'All right,' replied Mrs Fitzpatrick coolly. She
glided over to kiss Melissa goodbye, taking care
not to meet Frank's eyes. 'Have a good time,
darling.'

'Be back by eleven-thirty, Lissy,' instructed Mr
Fitzpatrick.

'I'll have her back by then for sure,' promised
Frank, wishing with all his heart his voice
wouldn't wobble so nervously.

'Don't trouble yourself too much, Frank!' said
Mrs Fitzpatrick hastily. 'If Ashley's at this dance
you're going to, I'm sure he wouldn't mind
seeing Melissa home. It's on his way, after all.'

Frank felt as though he'd been stung. He was
silent until they'd left the house and walked a
few blocks towards the town hall. As he strided
in the night beside the beautiful Melissa, he
wondered over the degrading scene. He had to
admit, he couldn't help wondering if Melissa had

deliberately set out to humiliate him in front of
her parents. Maybe she'd been laughing at him
the whole time? He sighed heavily. He'd really
wanted Melissa to be different. He'd hoped like
crazy she wasn't the same as all those snobby
kids; that she'd like him for himself and not
dismiss him out of hand just because he wasn't
rich and his father was a criminal. But it seemed
Melissa might be like the rest after all . . . or had
the whole thing been unintentional? He puzzled
over the possibilities, unable to discover the
answer.

'You're quiet . . .' Melissa said tentatively.

'Mmmm . . .' he answered. 'I was just thinking.'

They walked in the darkness silently. A few
seconds passed.

'Melissa?'

'Yes, Frank?'

'I don't think your parents liked me much.'

Melissa feigned surprise. 'What makes you think
that?'

Frank bit the bullet. He decided he had to know
the truth. 'Well . . . the things you said.' He
paused awkwardly. 'I wish you hadn't told them
about my father.'

Melissa cringed guiltily. She'd been wishing the exact same thing. 'I'm sorry, Frank, I didn't realise . . .' She was glad it was dark so he couldn't see her face blushing beetroot with the lie.

'Were you deliberately trying to humiliate me?' Frank asked quietly.

'No, Frank! No way!' Melissa lied again. 'I'm sorry, I just didn't think. I'd never do anything like that deliberately, honestly.'

Frank stopped and studied her pretty face under a neon street light. More than anything, he wanted to believe her. 'Okay,' he smiled gently. 'I believe you.'

Melissa smiled back. She'd never seen such a handsome guy. Ashley had nothing on Frank Morgan in the looks department. And those eyes.

'I'm sorry for thinking you did it deliberately,' apologized Frank.

'That's okay, I understand,' she replied, a knife twisting guiltily in her heart.

'It's just that, I don't know, it's bad enough to think that your father's in prison, without having people make fun of you for it,' he explained. 'I'd give anything to have a real family . . . a nice normal family where your dad yells sometimes, but it always ends up being okay, and you go on picnics and stuff. It's a bit like that with Tom and Pippa, my foster parents, but it's not the same if they're not your real family, you know?'

Melissa nodded, though she couldn't possibly know.

'And it's stuff like that that makes it all seem pretty unfair,' he continued, 'because you're already suffering enough, but everyone wants you to suffer some more. Do you understand what I mean?'

'Yes I do,' Melissa smiled softly up at his eyes. She longed to take Frank's hand, but she couldn't. She knew he thought she was lovely now, but he'd hate her in a couple of hours. Poor Frank, he'd had such a hard life. And he was so gorgeous . . . if only this whole thing hadn't started. But it was too late to back out now, far too late. Because she knew that right now Emily would be at Ashley Kieran's luxurious home, enlisting his help in the plan.

'She's my girlfriend.' Ashley thumped the table angrily. 'What's she going out with that pre-pubescent pauper for?'

Emily leaned forward confidentially. 'If you'd listen to me for a minute Ashley, I'll tell you.'

Ashley sighed angrily and leaned back against his chair. 'I'm all ears.'

'Well, she thinks you've been taking her for granted,' Emily lied, 'and Frank Morgan's been following her around like a pathetic little puppy for weeks. So she thought if she went to the dance with him, you'd sit up and take some notice, and she could turn him off her at the same time.'

'Are you sure that's why?' Ashley was still suspicious.

'Of course I'm sure. She told me!' Emily insisted. She lowered her voice so Ashley's parents, watching TV in the adjoining room, wouldn't hear their conversation.

'Where are you and your mates going tonight?'

'Below Zero.'

Emily was impressed. Ashley and his friends hung out at the hippest nightclub in the city. But they couldn't go there tonight, or the plan wouldn't work! 'Don't go there. Come to the Town Hall Dance.'

Ashley threw back his handsome head and snorted scornfully. 'You've got to be kidding! As if we'd be seen dead at a dance with a pack of teenyboppers.' He leaned forward angrily. 'And as if I'd be seen dead there when my girlfriend's with somebody else!'

'But that's the whole point!' Emily insisted. 'Frank Morgan's band is playing at the dance –.

'Huh! All the more reason not to go!' yelled Ashley.

'No, all the more reason to go!' sneered Emily wickedly. 'Melissa and me need your help with her plan to get Frank off her back . . . come to the dance and you'll love it!'

Ashley grinned. What were they up to? 'Yeah?'

'Yeah,' said Emily smugly. 'I promise. Now here's what we want you to do . . .'

Frank felt fantastic walking into the hall with Melissa Fitzpatrick by his side. It was his band, their gig, their night. And the most beautiful girl in the school was on his arm. He'd forgotten all about his earlier embarrassment. Tonight was going to be magic!

He led Melissa through the whispering teenagers, up the stairs to the backstage area, where Jimbo, Peabrain and Stud were setting up the equipment. He strolled over casually. 'Guys, you know Melissa don't you?'

'Yeah, sort of. Hi . . .'

'Hi . . .'

'G'day.'

The band shuffled awkwardly, trying to avoid Melissa's blue-eyed gaze. What was Frank playing at? She wasn't his type. She was probably only here for a laugh with her snobby friends. They could see that clear as day. Why couldn't Frank?

'This is The Remedial Class, Melissa. James, Geoff and Stephen,' smiled Frank proudly, completely unaware of the undertones.

'Hello,' Melissa said, smiling awkwardly. She felt uncomfortable and embarrassed. There was something about Frank's mates . . . they couldn't tell what she was up to, could they? She didn't know. But she did know one thing. She wanted to get away from their disapproving stares. Maybe this was how Frank had felt with her parents?

'I'll go out the front and let you get ready,' she told Frank. 'Good luck.'

'Thanks,' Frank smiled at her, stars in his eyes. 'I'll come and talk to you in the break.' He couldn't take his eyes off her as she disappeared through the backstage door.

The other guys exchanged unhappy glances.

125

Couldn't Frank see what he was letting himself in for?

'So where's that Ashley Kieran guy?' Stud asked pointedly.

'I think they've broken up,' Frank said defensively.

'That's not what I heard,' said Stud.

'Me either,' agreed Jimbo.

'I saw them together yesterday,' said Peabrain.

Frank felt his hackles rise. 'Okay, so what are you getting at?'

The ever-reasonable Jimbo did his best to be diplomatic. 'Look, I know you're pretty keen on her, Morgan, but she's not your type. You can tell a mile off.'

'She's not, mate. She's too snobby. Why's she going out with you?' interjected Peabrain.

'I'll tell you why,' snorted Stud. 'She's using him. She's laughing at him behind his back with all her stuck-up friends.'

Frank's face was white with fury. These jerks called themselves his mates! Who did they think they were? 'There's one word that describes you three morons,' he sneered. 'And that's jealous!' He picked up his guitar case. 'Come on. We've got a gig to play.'

The town hall was filling rapidly with teenagers from every one of the nearby high schools. Disco lights were flashing around the ceiling and the buzz of conversation was loud, as the volunteer bouncers and soft drink sellers prepared for the inevitable onslaught.

Already groups of giggling girls walked flirtatiously past boys they usually only saw in the playground. Everyone wore the one hip outfit they'd managed to wangle out of their parents for their birthday or Christmas present. The atmosphere was alive with excitement as the youthful patrons started gearing up for a really good time.

There was a buzz around the hall as kids discussed the band, The Remedial Class. No-one knew much about them – just that they were local kids given a break by the grown-ups who'd organized the dance. Everyone hoped they wouldn't play daggy old covers or poxy new originals you couldn't dance to.

Into this vibrant scene from backstage walked Melissa, just in time to see Emily, with Ashley and several of his closest mates, saunter coolly into the hall. The scheme was working like clockwork so far. So why did Melissa feel so awful?

The buzz of conversation reached a crescendo with the arrival of Ashley Kieran. People were amazed. These guys normally wouldn't be seen dead at a no alcohol dance! The Remedial Class must really be something, to drag the big men away from the city. Everyone immediately felt part of something more hip and exciting than they would have dared hope. Being at the town hall tonight was the coolest place to be, obviously. They couldn't wait for the band to start.

They didn't have long to wait. Within a few minutes the sounds of instruments tuning up and nervous coughing came from behind the stage curtain.

At the same time strong arms gripped a tense Melissa around her shapely waist. 'Thought I wasn't paying you enough attention eh?' whispered Ashley Kieran. 'How's this for starters?' And he swept her into a passionate kiss. Hundreds of female eyes looked on enviously.

'This little wimp's going to regret the day he ever asked you out,' Ashley promised when he finally released her.

Melissa smoothed her hair, embarrassed by Ashley's passionate display. 'Couldn't we just leave together or something?' she suggested, anxious to avoid Frank further humiliation. 'That way he'd get the message.'

'No way!' declared Ashley. 'There's about ten people here really looking forward to rubbing that little jerk's nose in the dirt.' He chuckled. 'Especially me!'

Melissa didn't get the chance to argue any further. At that moment the stage curtains drew back to reveal the band. Kids clapped and cheered, ready for raging.

'Hi. We're the Remedial Class,' Frank said, smiling into the microphone. 'We hope everybody has a really good time tonight.'

'Some of us will have a better time than others!' Ashley whispered snidely into Melissa's ear. She found herself wishing he'd go away.

There were more cheers and claps from the crowd as The Remedial Class launched into their first number. Melissa was pleasantly surprised. They were great! The dance floor filled almost immediately, and those who weren't bopping on the floor were tapping their feet to the catchy tune. Ashley pulled Melissa onto the dance floor. Emily bopped beside them with Ashley's best friend, Glenn Chaplin. She hated to admit it, but Frank Morgan actually had an okay voice. Well, she chuckled to herself, he'd be singing a different tune by the time tonight was over!

She studied his face from down on the dance floor, and was pleased to see him notice Melissa and Ashley with dismay. She tapped Melissa on the shoulder and hissed into her ear. 'He's watching! Quick! Go for it!'

Melissa started writhing sexily in front of Ashley, throwing her arms around his neck and leaning close, smiling up at him seductively. She was surprised to find herself wishing it was Frank she was embracing. She'd love to throw her arms around that neck instead . . . but it was too late now. All the kids would dump her if she chickened out at this stage. And Melissa couldn't stand the thought of not being popular. She kissed Ashley passionately, and he held on to her possessively, smiling triumphantly up at Frank.

Frank tried to keep his mind on the song, but he was finding it incredibly difficult. He couldn't believe his eyes. There she was, right in front of him, throwing herself all over Ashley when everyone knew she'd arrived with Frank. She was trying to humiliate him – again – and she was succeeding. He felt a pain in his heart that hurt so badly he was sure it would soon stop beating. And there was that creepy Emily Green, smiling bitchily up at him. Frank was devastated. He'd thought this was going to be a special night for him and Melissa. He should have known better!

Ashley Kieran nodded his head in his cronies' direction, as though giving some kind of signal.

Immediately catcalls started. Strategically placed on every side of the hall, they hassled and harrassed the band with raucous complaints.

'Who are these pathetic jerks?!'

'Get 'em off!'

'They stink!'

'I've heard monkeys play better music!'

'What is this? Music or torture?!'

Frank and the guys tried valiantly to ignore the cruel cries. The other three exchanged anxious glances. What was happening? But Frank knew exactly was happening. It was written all over Emily Green's vicious smirk.

Ashley released Melissa and started slow clapping. 'Get Off! Get Off!' he called rhythmically. His followers immediately took up the chant, and the band was almost drowned out by their volume.

Elsewhere in the hall people were puzzled. These were the coolest guys in town, demanding that the band stop playing. Maybe The Remedial Class wasn't so good after all? The more impressionable kids started chanting along with Ashley and his gang. 'Get off! Get off! Get off!'

Then some other kids with minds of their own,

who recognized the band's true ability, tried in vain to give them support.

'Leave them alone! They're great!' they yelled. 'Stay on! Keep going!'

But Ashley and his gang shouted over them. 'Get Off! Get Off! Get Off!' they demanded. They said it again and again, louder and louder, stronger and stronger, drowning everyone out.

Up on stage, Frank tried not to react. But he couldn't help it. The music could hardly be heard anymore. Stud, Jimbo and Peabrain were looking more worried with every passing second. Frank felt fury rising in his chest. How dare they – these stuck-up rich kids who thought they were a breed apart? How dare they try and ruin his night just because he was different? He was tired of it. Tired of all the jibes about being dumb, tired of the innuendo about his father, tired of falling for girls like Melissa, tired of being a laughing stock. But most of all, he was very, very angry.

Before he even knew what he was doing, he'd thrown his guitar down and leaped from the stage, surprising Ashley Kieran with a deft right hook. Ashley wobbled momentarily, then set about defending himself with a series of heavy punches. Ashley's burly friends joined the fray, spoiling for a fight. Then Stud, Jimbo and even

Peabrain, jumped from the stage to help defend Frank. Supporters of both sides joined in. Before anyone knew what was happening, the whole hall had erupted in an ugly brawl.

Emily moved quickly away from the madness, dragging Melissa with her. Her face was a mask of triumph. 'We did it!' She laughed maliciously as punches were thrown and people injured in every corner of the hall. 'It's worked out even better than we thought! They're going to bash Frank Morgan into a pulp! Look, Melissa! Look!'

'I don't want to look!' Melissa yelled desperately. 'I wish we'd never done it! He doesn't deserve it. I hate you, Emily Green! I hate you!' And she ran from the town hall, sobbing.

chapter six

Bobby Simpson felt fantastic. In two hours time she'd be Bobby Morgan, married to the world's most wonderful guy.

Wow, what a day! Her heart glowed with happiness as she slipped her wedding dress over her head, helped by her chief bridesmaid and foster sister, Carly.

'Well, I hate to say it, but you look pretty nice,' grinned Carly, doing up Bobby's zip. 'Pretty nice' was an understatement. Bobby was a knockout in a strapless ivory raw silk gown with a ruched bodice and a full skirt that swished and swirled, thanks to black tulle petticoats! She'd virtually designed it herself. It was elegant, original – and very Bobby.

'Kill me with praise, why don't ya?' retorted the bride. 'How about a –'

She caught a glimpse of herself in the mirror, and her flippant words stuck in her throat. She couldn't believe the beautiful bride staring back at her was ... well, her. Carly stood behind her, smiling into the mirror.

'Frank's a pretty lucky guy I reckon,' she said sincerely.

'Not half as lucky as me.' Bobby was surprised to find herself on the edge of tears.

'I don't know ...' considered Carly, who looked rather lovely herself in emerald green silk. She bent down, fluffing up Bobby's black tulle petticoats. 'When you think of everything Frank's been through, it's a miracle this day ever came.'

Bobby nodded pensively as she gazed into the mirror. She smiled tenderly at the thought of her fiance. 'He's always saying coming to Summer Bay was the best thing that ever happened to him. Even when you all first arrived he was really aggro, wasn't he?'

Carly nodded. 'Yeah. He had a pretty tough time in the city. So did Tom and Pippa, all the worrying they did about him.'

Bobby sank down on to the bed.

'Get up!' demanded Carly. 'You'll crumple your dress!'

Bobby shrugged. 'Too bad. Frankie-Boy will still love me.' She looked at Carly curiously. 'He's never told me much about all that stuff. I knew

135

he wasn't happy before you came here to Hicks-ville, but I didn't know Tom and Pippa were freaked out about him.'

Carly surveyed herself in the mirror, fiddling with her tight blonde curls. 'Yeah, well Pippa once told me that for a few years her and Tom felt really guilty about the way they'd handled Frank. They thought they'd ruined his life.'

Bobby considered this interesting revelation. 'This is going to sound soppy,' she ventured, 'but a person's allowed to be a bit over the top of their wedding day aren't they?'

'Yeah,' Carly grinned. 'I s'pose.'

'I'm going to share Frank's future with him,' Bobby said, a bit embarrassed, 'but I want to share his past with him too. So there's no secrets or anything – you know?'

Carly nodded, refraining from the temptation to tease her foster sister. She knew what she was hearing was coming straight from the heart.

'You've known him a lot longer than I have,' said Bobby. 'Tell me why he was so unhappy.'

'Do you really want to hear?' asked Carly.

'I love him,' said Bobby, her heart filled with pride. 'I want to know everything about him.'

*

Knock knock knock!

The rapping on the front door was loud and insistent, drowning out the television. Tom and Pippa exchanged a startled glance.

'Who the hell could that be?' asked Tom in annoyance.

'Only one way to find out I suppose,' said Pippa, puzzled.

Tom strode to the front door followed closely by Pippa, calling out, 'All right! We're coming!' as the loud rapping continued, relentless.

He opened the door to find a bloodied, bruised Frank standing silent and morose on the doorstep, accompanied by a policeman. Pippa's hand went straight to her mouth.

'Mr and Mrs Fletcher?' the policeman asked officiously.

'Yes,' said a troubled Tom. 'What is it? Come in.'

Frank and the policeman stepped into the hall.

'Are you all right, Frank?' Pippa asked anxiously, eyeing his obviously fight-induced injuries. Frank remained silent.

'I'm Constable Simon Campbell from Burwood Police Station. There was a brawl at the town hall dance tonight, started by your foster son here.'

137

Pippa and Tom stared at Frank in alarm. What had possessed him to start a brawl?

'Luckily the lad he attacked isn't pressing charges, but I'd like you to impress upon the boy the fact that he's not allowed near that young fella again. He certainly isn't listening to me.'

Frank's face was a morose mask.

'Have you got anything to say for yourself, Frank?' Tom asked sternly.

'Hasn't opened his mouth since we arrived at the hall,' said Constable Campbell. 'Apparently there was some provocation, according to a lot of the youngsters there, but that's still no excuse to start an all-out fight.'

'Of course not,' agreed Tom.

'We've let him off with a warning this time,' said the policeman, preparing to leave, 'but next time we'll come down on him like a ton of bricks, I promise you.'

'There won't be a next time,' said Tom.

'Well, I hope not,' the policeman replied piously. 'We've got enough on our plate without pulling yobbo teenagers apart. I think a bit more parental guidance would make a big difference.'

'Thanks for the advice,' Tom said icily, 'but we'll do our job and you do yours, eh?'

'Goodbye, Constable,' said Pippa politely, opening the door. 'Thank you for bringing him home.'

'Goodbye,' said the Constable. He turned and strode off into the darkness. Pippa closed the door firmly behind him. Tom turned to Frank angrily. 'Now what the hell is all this about?'

Frank stared straight ahead silently. Pippa bit her lip. His injuries were fairly minor, but they still needed attending to. But it seemed Tom was too angry to notice. 'I said – what's all this about starting some damn brawl?'

There was a tense silence, then Frank spoke. 'Don't worry about it. It's over,' he muttered darkly.

'Well – he's found his tongue!' said Tom sarcastically, ignoring Pippa's warning glance. 'Would you like to tell me why it happened?'

Frank stared straight through Tom as though he were transparent. 'No. I wouldn't.' He started heading for the stairs. 'I'm going to bed.'

Tom made to move after him, but Pippa grabbed her husband's arm. 'Can I help you get cleaned up, Frank?' she offered gently. 'Do you want some disinfectant?'

'No,' Frank said coldly. 'I'll fix it.' And he disappeared up the stairs.

Tom and Pippa went to the kitchen, confused and very concerned. 'Why would he have started a fight, Pip?' Tom puzzled as Pippa filled the kettle. 'He hasn't done anything like that for years.'

'I don't know,' Pippa sighed. 'But it doesn't look like he's got any intention of telling us.' She shivered involuntarily. Tom walked over and put his arm around her shoulder. 'Did you see the way he was looking at us?'

'Straight through us, like he used to when he first arrived.'

'We haven't seen that look for so long Tom,' said Pippa miserably. 'Why now? What's wrong?'

Tom pursed his lips thoughtfully. 'I don't know, but I wouldn't mind betting it's got something to do with this Melissa.'

'Probably,' agreed Pippa. 'But what?'

Tom shrugged his shoulders hopelessly. 'Who could say? You're right about one thing though. He's got no intention of telling us.' He paused, remembering Frank's sullen silence. 'It was like he didn't trust us anymore, wasn't it?'

'Like that look he used to have on his dear little face when his dreams were the only thing he thought he could depend on,' agreed Pippa sadly.

They sat in silence. Minutes passed.

'This isn't good, Pip,' Tom said finally. 'In fact, it's pretty damn disturbing.' Pippa nodded. 'Maybe we've messed up somewhere?' He sighed. 'If he still won't talk to us tomorrow, we'll have to call in the Department.'

The next morning an earnest young man strode up the street towards the Fletchers' house. Tarquin Pierce straightened his tie a touch nervously. He hadn't been a case worker with the Department of Youth and Community Services for very long, and this was one of his first major cases. He cleared his throat as he walked up the Fletcher's front path. He wanted so badly to be a good case worker, to really understand what made these kids tick. He'd had an unhappy childhood himself, so he was really keen to help kids like Frank turn their lives around. The Department had been surprised to get the worried call from Tom and Pippa this morning. They'd all thought Frank Morgan had been progressing so well. Obviously something had gone horribly wrong. He knocked on the door. But what was it? Tarquin hoped Frank would feel free to confide in him.

'I'm not going back to school,' Frank told Tarquin

141

defiantly. They were in his room with the door closed.

'Why not?'

'Because I'm old enough to make my own decisions, and that's what I've decided. That's why.'

Tarquin was disturbed by the depth of Frank's bitterness. He'd already met many angry kids in his job, but never one this sullenly resigned to a solitary life. It was like Frank had given up on everyone except himself. But the irony was, he didn't like himself either. And that left him with no-one. Tarquin found the situation very sad.

'But what will you do?' asked Tarquin, restraining himself from advising Frank to the contrary.

'I've got a band going,' Frank said defensively. 'I'm going to work full-time on that.'

Tarquin bit his tongue, reminding himself that the most important part of his job was simply listening.

'What's your band called?' he asked.

'The Remedial Class,' answered Frank suspiciously, unsure of whether Tarquin's interest was genuine.

'Good name,' Tarquin commented. 'What kind of stuff do you play? Covers?'

'No,' Frank replied. 'Mostly originals. I write them.'

'Really?' said Tarquin. 'I'm impressed. I tried to write a few songs a long time ago, but I was never any good at it.'

Frank searched the young man's face intently. He was the first adult who'd ever shown any real interest in the band. Oh, Tom and Pippa listened when he told them stuff, but they didn't really understand. This guy obviously did. Or did he – asked the cynical side of Frank's brain. Maybe he was just putting it on? He looked at Tarquin again. No. He could tell he wasn't. The guy was actually interested.

Tarquin watched Frank sizing him up. He hoped he passed the test. He liked this young man, and he wanted to help him.

'But why do you have to leave school now?' he asked tentatively. 'Why can't you stay at least 'til the end of Year Ten?'

Frank met his gaze with eyes almost blazing in their hostility. 'I'll tell you why,' he began, 'then you can tell Tom and Pippa, and everyone will know.' He took a deep breath and all his insecurities and unhappy memories came flooding out, in a relentless flow of words that stunned Tarquin Pierce with their sadness. 'Because I'm the laughing stock of the school, that's why. Because I'm a dumb no-hoper who never gets good marks, who doesn't live with his parents – who doesn't even know where his mother is – but I know where my father is, don't I? And so does everyone else in the school – he's in gaol for drug pushing! People pretend they like me, then they walk all over me, and every time I think I'm getting somewhere I get kicked in the face like at the dance last night! I'm no good for anything except being laughed at! I'm a loser, a jerk, a no-hoper, a dag – and I always will be!'

Frank's eyes burned into Tarquin Pierce, daring him to deny it.

'It's very unfortunate,' Tarquin told Tom and Pippa downstairs a little later. 'The poor fella has absolutely no self-esteem. He's convinced he's the lowest of the low.'

'I know,' Pippa said desperately. 'But what can we do about it?'

Tarquin took a sip of his coffee, then sighed thoughtfully. 'You've got to try and talk him into staying on at school.'

Tom snorted. 'That's a lot easier said than done, mate. We thought we were in there with a chance for a while, but now this Melissa girl's done the dirty on him he doesn't want to know about it.'

'If I could get my hands on her I'd wring her nasty little neck!' exclaimed Pippa angrily.

'I know how you feel,' Tarquin Pierce smiled, 'but obviously that's no solution. All the frustration and resentment that's destroying Frank at the moment is the culmination of years of being teased in the playground, feeling like a second-class citizen, all of that. If he leaves now to try and get a band happening, it'll only make things worse. How many bands make it to the big time? One in a thousand?'

Tom nodded. 'If that.'

'And those one in a thousand that do make it, spend a lot of back-breaking, financially un-rewarding years slogging their guts out in second-rate pubs . . .'

'It's no life . . .' agreed Pippa.

'I honestly believe, and I speak for the Department too,' said Tarquin, 'that a move like that would end up wiping out what little self-esteem he does have.'

'I've got to agree with you there,' said Tom.

'Please,' asked Tarquin, 'do your utmost to get him to stay at school. If he applies himself to those extra two years of study it'll give him a really valuable feeling of self-worth, not to mention a solid education. A boy of Frank's background needs that very badly.'

'We know . . .' Pippa chewed her lip miserably. 'But it's not only his education, is it? He feels so alone, so isolated . . . what can we do to solve that?'

Tarquin cleared his throat and put down his coffee cup. 'That was another thing I wanted to talk to you about.'

'A foster sister?'

Frank had hardly touched his evening meal. He pushed his plate away, surprised at the question he'd just been asked.

'Would you like that?' Pippa asked again nervously.

Frank shrugged his shoulders. 'I don't care. Whatever you reckon.'

Tom and Pippa exchanged a tense glance.

'The Department's got somebody in mind,' said Tom, smiling a touch too casually. 'Her name's Carly Morris. She's fourteen – is it, Pip?'

'Thirteen,' corrected Pippa.

'Yeah, right,' said Tom. 'Anyway, she's been pretty badly treated by her dad, from all accounts. Seems she could do with a nice stable family life, especially a big brother . . .' He looked at Frank hopefully. Frank thought about it. He wouldn't mind having a younger sister. Might be fun. A younger sister who looked up to him. Yeah, at least she'd never call him a jerk.

'It'd be nice to have a foster sister, wouldn't it, Frank?' enthused Pippa. 'You mightn't feel so alone then. You'd have another –'

'Another loser to hang around with?' Frank interrupted bitterly.

'You know that's not what I meant! said Pippa. 'You're not a loser!'

Tom decided the time had arrived for a firm approach to his foster son's problems. 'And while we're on the subject, the only way to prove to yourself that you're not a loser is to stay at school and do your HSC.'

'No way!' declared Frank. 'I'm never going back there!'

'Listen, mate, 'said Tom firmly, 'we know you've had a tough time of it, but it's like riding a horse. You've got to climb straight back on and keep going. Do you want those stupid kids to think you're too gutless to face them?'

Frank sat silently, obviously affected by his foster father's argument.

147

'Well, do you?' Tom persevered. 'Do you want to give them the satisfaction of knowing they've beaten you?'

Frank moaned inwardly. He knew Tom was right. How could he let Ashley Kieran get away with it? But he didn't want to go back and face the sneering scumbags . . . he didn't want to . . . he didn't want to . . .

'What would you do between now and the end of the year anyway?' asked Pippa reasonably. 'The other boys in the band won't be leaving until Year Ten is over, will they?'

Frank made a snap decision. He didn't want to give Ashley and Emily the pleasure of victory, but more important than that, he didn't want to disappoint Tom and Pippa. They were the only thing he had going for him.

'All right, I'll go back to school on Monday,' he announced, 'but the minute Year Ten finishes, the band takes over!' He pushed his chair away from the table and headed up the stairs.

Left alone, Tom and Pippa exchanged a rueful glance.

'Well, that's half a victory I guess,' said Pippa. 'But how will we get him to stay on for two years?'

Tom's brow was furrowed. He was deep in thought. Finally he spoke. 'I can think of a way,' he said. 'I don't like to do it – in fact I hate it – but I think it's probably the only way.'

The following night a few kilometres away, the bruised and battered Remedial Class held another secret meeting minus one member.

'I feel bad about Frank not being here,' said Peabrain.

'Me too,' agreed Jimbo, nursing a black eye.

'Don't start that crap again!' admonished Stud. 'Use your heads. How can we have a meeting about him if he's here?'

'I didn't know this meeting was about Morgan,' said Jimbo.

'Yes you did,' accused the long-suffering Stud, 'even if you're pretending you didn't.'

Jimbo and Peabrain were silent. Stud was spot-on, of course. They'd known full well this meeting, like the last one, was all about Frank; but they hadn't wanted to admit to themselves they were discussing their leader's worthiness.

'I had another 'phone call this arvo,' announced Stud. 'From Beaumont High. They've cancelled our dance gig.'

'Geez, no,' moaned Jimbo. 'That's the third can-
cellation since –'

'Since Friday night,' finished Stud. 'They said
they heard we started a brawl. They don't want
a band with a bad name playing at their dance.'

'Bummer!' groaned Peabrain.

'Triple bummer,' said Stud meaningfully. 'Now
what I say is, I didn't start the brawl, you didn't
start the brawl Jimbo, and neither did you Peabrain.'

'Fair go, Stud, we know who started it,' said
Jimbo.

'Yeah,' agreed Peabrain.

'That's right!' said Stud. 'And I say now we've
definitely got to dump him from the band!'

Jimbo and Peabrain exchanged troubled glances.
They'd known this was coming, but they still
didn't like it. 'We can't do that! He's our mate!'
cried Jimbo.

'Huh! Some mate!' snorted Stud. 'He doesn't
listen when we try and help him, then he starts
a fight and gives the whole band a bad name.'

'They were hasslin' him Stud. Real loud. You
heard 'em,' pointed out Peabrain.

'Yeah,' admitted Stud, 'but Morgan couldn't control himself. He's trouble, with a Capital T. That's the point I'm making.'

Jimbo and Peabrain were contemplating Stud's worrying claim, when Mrs Clarke knocked on his bedroom door. 'Stephen?'

'Yeah Mum?'

Mrs Clarke opened the door. A tall man with dark hair and a kind face stood beside her. 'Mr Fletcher's here. Frank's foster father. He wants to have a talk to you.'

Tom walked into the room, smiling thanks at Mrs Clarke as she closed the door behind her. He felt badly for what he was about to ask. He hoped Frank's mates would understand, but he couldn't blame them if they didn't.

'Hello, fellas.'

'Hi, Mr Fletcher.'

Stud, Jimbo and Peabrain exchanged a curious glance. What was he doing here?

'I just wanted to have a word with you about Frank.'

'Yeah?' asked Stud defensively. Maybe Mr Fletcher was going to blame them for the fight?

'Mind if I sit down?'

'Sure . . .'

Tom took a seat at Stud's homework desk. Then he cleared his throat. 'It's like this, fellas . . . sometimes being a mate, and a foster dad, means doing things that don't seem very nice at the time, but things that you have to do for your friend's, or foster son's, good in the long-run.' He paused. 'Do you understand what I'm getting at?'

He studied the three blank faces in front of him. They obviously didn't.

'Not really,' admitted Jimbo.

Tom sighed. He really hated to do this. 'Well you blokes have had a very different life from Frank. You've always had your family around you, but Frank's missed out on a lot of that stuff. His life was so unstable when he was a little kid, that me and his foster mother feel the thing he needs most in life is a bit of stability. Fair enough?'

The three boys shrugged non-committally. Tom pressed on.

'We think that leaving school and going into the band full-time would be a bad move for Frank in the long-run.' He sighed. 'We've tried to talk him into staying on, but he won't listen to us. So for Frank's good, I'm asking you blokes to drop him from the band.'

There. He'd done it. He'd done what he thought was right for Frank, but it certainly didn't make him feel like a good father. In fact, Tom felt like a double-crossing creep.

The boys stared at each other in amazement. How could Frank's foster father ask them to do such a thing? This guy must be a real scumbag!

'I know it sounds horrible, fellas,' Tom finished awkwardly. 'But I promise you it's for his own good. He'll thank you for it in the long-run.'

Jimbo and Peabrain remained impassive. Only Stud seemed swayed by Tom's arguments.

'I dunno Mr Fletcher . . .'

Tom stood up and walked towards the door. 'I know you blokes will want to discuss this on your own.' He paused. 'Look, I realize it probably sounds a bit rough, but Pippa and me wouldn't ask you to do it unless we were sure it was the best thing for Frank, I promise you that. And you can choose to disagree, whatever you reckon. I just thought I'd ask. See you later.'

'Yeah, see ya,' muttered the guys as Tom left, closing the door behind him. They exchanged incredulous looks.

'Some foster father!' scoffed Jimbo.

'Yeah!' agreed Peabrain. 'Wanting us to dump on Frank.'

'He's right,' said Stud.

'Yeah, well I knew you'd say that,' retorted Jimbo angrily. 'You've been trying to make us get rid of poor Frank for about a week.'

'I want the best thing for him,' insisted Stud, 'just like Mr Fletcher does.'

'How can dumping him be good for him?' asked Peabrain, annoyed.

'Because it is, that's all,' declared Stud. 'He needs the sterility.'

'Stability!' snorted Jimbo.

'Whatever,' said Stud. 'It's true. Think about it guys. Do you want more gigs like last Friday night?'

Jimbo and Peabrain didn't reply.

'If you don't then we've got to get rid of Morgan.'

They thought for a moment, then Jimbo spoke. 'He's our mate,' he said loyally. 'Let's give him one more chance.'

'Yeah, one more chance,' agreed Peabrain.

Stud crossed his arms sulkily. 'All right,' he allowed. 'But one more hassle and he's out. Right?'

Jimbo and Peabrain frowned at each other. They hated to do it, but . . .

'All right.'

The next day Frank felt his body burning, as eyes bored into him from all over the playground. He hated being back in this hole of a place. Why had he let Tom and Pippa talk him into staying 'til the end of the year? Emily Green was over there, laughing at him, her eyes glowing with malice. Ashley Kieran was sneering with his mates underneath a tree, and Melissa Fitzpatrick stood nearby, carefully avoiding Frank's eyes. He tried to saunter past carelessly, but he knew he hadn't fooled anybody. Then he spotted Jimbo, Peabrain and Stud hanging out at the end of the quadrangle. They were like an oasis at the end of a desert. He headed straight for his mates, wishing he could wear blinkers like a horse to avoid the stares from all other directions. He focused on the band, and what the future would be. Fame and fortune here they come! No-one would laugh at him then.

'Hey, guys!' he greeted his friends with forced cheeriness.

'G'day, Morgan,' they replied. He didn't notice their downcast eyes. He was too busy trying to convince himself, and them, that he felt great.

'What's happening?'

'Not much,' replied Stud.

'Not much?!' exclaimed Frank. 'This band is going to be the biggest thing since U2, and you're saying not much is happening?!'

Stud, Jimbo and Peabrain exchanged awkward glances.

'Got to get to the end of the year first,' said Jimbo.

'Yeah – but once we're out of this dump, I give us a week before we sign a recording contract!' enthused Frank. He continued on with brittle enthusiasm, trying not to notice Emily Green heading towards him. 'And I give us a year before we're filling up the Wembley Stadium in London!'

Jimbo met Peabrain's eyes. They were actually thinking the same thing as his. What was Frank acting so weird about? He was off his tree!

'We'll have to make sure we get a good manager, though,' declared Frank. ''Cause sometimes they rip bands off. Wouldn't want a couple of million to go astray before our eighteenth birthdays.'

Stud's eyes bored into Jimbo. He pulled a face, as if to say, 'What did I tell you?'

'Hey guys we're on our way!' Frank almost yelled in his desperate enthusiasm. 'We're going to be the next Beatles!'

Jimbo felt uncomfortable. He couldn't explain why – well, yes he could. He was starting to think Stud might be right about Frank getting out of control. He wanted to get away from Stud's significant stares, and he had to admit, from Frank's fake enthusiasm too. He caught Peabrain's eye. He could see his big mate felt the same.

'Got to go,' Jimbo said, staring at the ground. 'Get ready for class.'

'Yeah, me come too,' said Peabrain, glad of the excuse.

Frank intercepted their glances with alarm. Surely his mates weren't deserting him too? They couldn't. They were the only thing he had – the band, and Tom and Pippa. But maybe he was imagining it? He looked at their faces. They refused to meet his eyes. He knew he wasn't.

And suddenly, before Jimbo and Peabrain could leave, all Frank needed – Emily! She came sidling up to him with a bitchy smile on her freckly face, determined to make him even more miserable. 'Surprised to see you here, derro!' she cackled.

'Get lost, Green!' yelled Jimbo menacingly.

'Shut-up!' smirked Emily viciously. She was determined to make Frank pay. Melissa didn't like her anymore – the group had dropped her. That meant Frank Morgan had not only knocked her back, but lost all her friends for her too. It didn't occur to Emily to realize that she'd done it to herself, through her vicious spitefulness. All she thought about was revenge.

'You must be even more stupid than you look, coming back here when everyone hates your guts!' she yelled at Frank.

Over underneath the tree, Melissa Fitzpatrick watched the confrontation tensely. Ashley Kieran followed her gaze. His eyes narrowed. 'What are you looking at?' he asked threateningly.

'None of your business,' she retorted. She tried to move away, but Ashley held her arm in a vice-like grip. He coldn't bear to think that she still had a thing for that derro Frank Morgan. 'Keep your eyes off him!' he warned.

'I'm worried about what Emily's saying,' said Melissa. 'Frank's already been through enough.'

Ashley's grip on her arm tightened. 'Why don't you worry about me for once? I'm the one he attacked.'

'Only because you were stirring him!' yelled Melissa. 'Let go of me!' She pulled herself roughly from his grasp and started heading across the playground, calling out behind her 'Consider yourself dropped!'

Meanwhile, Frank was trying hard to restrain himself. Every fibre in his body urged him to bash in Emily's face as she continued her relentless tirade.

'Bet you'd like to get Ashley good and proper,' taunted Emily, 'but you're not allowed near him, are you? You'll go to gaol if you do – just like your good-for-nothing father!'

'Shut up about my father!' yelled Frank with an intensity that shocked his mates. He advanced towards her threateningly. 'Just shut up about my father!' he yelled, almost beserk. 'You ugly, freckled-faced pig! Shut up! Shut up! Shut up!'

He raised his fist to hit her, but Jimbo and Peabrain leapt behind him and grabbed his arms. He struggled against them. Emily jumped back in fright, the satisfied smile wiped from her face. And then Melissa arrived to vent her fury on her former friend.

'You should have let him hit her,' she said to Jimbo. 'She deserves it. She's a bitch. She's just tried to ruin Frank's life and make me unhappy as well. She started the whole thing.'

Emily listened silently, ashen-faced, as Melissa turned on her furiously. 'Why can't you leave people alone? Just 'cause you're horrible and no-one wants to go out with you, you try to ruin everyone else's life! I hate you, Emily Green! Everyone hates you! I never want to see you again! Never!'

A rasping breath rose in Emily's throat. She put her hand to her mouth and ran away, sobbing. The boys jeered behind her at her degradation. That is, all the boys except Frank. His face was a stony mask as they released his arms. Melissa looked at him beseechingly. 'I'm sorry Frank, I'm so sorry. Will you forgive me, please?'

The other guys looked around awkwardly. Maybe Melissa could be stuck-up sometimes, but they had to admit that she was gorgeous. And when she looked as sorry as this, they knew they'd find it impossible to be angry. But Frank found no such thing.

'I'll never forgive you,' he said, his voice like ice. 'I don't care what you do. I don't care what you think of me. I hate you. You're just like all the others. I never want to see you again – so just piss off!'

Melissa bit her lip in fright, but she told herself she deserved it. And she didn't want to give up on Frank yet. 'Please, Frank, I'm sorry. I've broken it off with Ashley, I've –'

But Frank strode towards her, drowning out her plea with his scream. 'I said – PISS OFF!'

'I'm sorry, Frank!' Melissa cried as she turned on her heel and fled. Tears streamed down her beautiful face.

The Remedial Class stood silently, unsure of what to say next. Frank stared at his friends defiantly, his face filled with hatred directed towards the whole world.

'That was a bit rough, Morgan,' Stud said at last.

'I don't care,' retorted Frank. 'I hate everyone except you guys. Everyone.' He took a deep breath and changed the subject. 'I'm getting out of this hole. Wanna come?'

The other boys didn't reply. They seemed embarrassed. Then Stud broke the silence. 'Nah. Reckon I'd better hang around today,' he said.

Jimbo agreed instantly. 'Me too.'

Frank looked at Peabrain. The big guy shrugged his shoulders awkwardly. 'Yeah. Me too.'

Frank felt the world falling out from beneath him. But he refused to face it. 'Fair enough,' he said, his smile strained. 'Might go see a few record companies about a contract. Tell you all about it at band practice.'

The other boys nodded dumbly. Frank turned and walked away. Left alone at the furthest end of the quadrangle, Stud, Jimbo and Peabrain looked at each other glumly, then looked after Frank. Finally Stud spoke. 'What did I tell you, guys? Trouble with a capital T.'

Jimbo thought for a moment. He felt awful, but . . . he looked at Peabrain, who nodded sadly. Then he turned to Stud regretfully. 'Yeah, mate. We'll have to do it.'

Tom and Pippa were watching television when Frank arrived home that evening. He strode into the loungeroom, stony-faced, his eyes hiding any emotional turmoil taking place underneath.

'We were wondering when you'd get home,' smiled Pippa.

'Got a spot of news,' said Tom.

'Yeah? So have I,' replied Frank impassively.

'Ours first,' said Pippa. She took Tom's hand and held it tight. Carly Morris is coming to live with us in a couple of weeks, so you'll have a foster sister. Isn't that terrific?'

'Yeah,' answered Frank, unenthusiastically.

Tom searched his foster son's face for clues of what his day had held. He felt lousy about asking the fellas to drop Frank from the band.

162

He had to admit he was rather hoping they'd decided not to do so.

'What's your news?' asked Pippa.

'Well,' Frank told them evenly, his voice betraying no emotion, 'I've been dropped from The Remedial Class. They don't want to know about me anymore – just like everyone else. So I'll be staying at school, 'cause I got nothing else to do. Happy?'

He stalked upstairs, leaving a guilty Tom and Pippa behind to trouble over their actions.

'Did you see how bad the poor bloke felt, Pip?' Tom remarked. 'I feel about as low as a snake.'

Pippa nodded. 'I know, but we have to remember, we did it for Frank's good,' she comforted her husband.

'Yeah?' Suddenly Tom was uncertain. 'Well I sure hope it works out that way.'

Four years later in sleepy Summer Bay, Carly helped Bobby pull her black tulle wrap around her creamy shoulders. Bobby had become totally lost in the sadness of Frank's adolescence. She was going to make the rest of his life everything his teenage years had not been. Carly thought back to those times again.

'You think I'm a mess now!' she smiled, 'You should have seen me when I first came to live with Tom and Pippa. I was a wreck – I didn't trust anyone or anything, I was sulky and horrible.' She brushed a speck from her elegant emerald green bridesmaid's dress. 'But Frank was fantastic to me. He was the big brother little girls dream about.'

'Yeah, I bet,' Bobby smiled at the thought.

'But he was really unhappy with everything else, you know?' continued Carly. 'He hated school, and he was so bitter that he wouldn't let anyone get close to him – except at home. She paused for a moment, remembering times past. 'He was so good to me, and then Lyn and Sal. Pippa told me that home was like an oasis to him, you know what I mean?'

Bobby nodded.

'Tom and Pippa felt awful because he hated school so much and he got lousy marks,' said Carly. 'And when school was finished he couldn't find a job. For a while they thought they'd really wrecked things for him. The Remedial Class was starting to get pretty well-known around the city, and Frank was, well, nowhere.' She paused to brush and fiddle with the bride's full skirt.

164

'That must have been why he had it in for Stevo at the start,' Bobby deduced.

'Yeah,' agreed Carly. 'It was. He hated brainy kids! Who could blame him? Anyway, when Tom came home and told us he'd lost his job, and we started talking about moving up here, Frank decided he may as well come, 'cause he had nothing to leave behind. He said that even if it was a hick town, at least he'd be with the family.' She smiled at Bobby warmly, past tensions forgotten. 'Turned out to be the best move he ever made.'

Bobby smiled back. 'For me too.'

There was silence as the two girls lost themselves in thought. Seconds passed, then the spell was broken by exuberant rapping on the bedroom door. 'Come on! Let's go! Let's go!' Sally cried excitedly from the hallway.

'We've got a wedding to get to!' called Tom.

epilogue

Frank's eyes brimmed with tears as the moving strains of the Wedding March filled Summer Bay's sandstone church. He turned to Pippa, beaming proudly in the front pew, and realized what he'd always known. Tom and Pippa were the best parents any guy could ever have. The fact that they weren't his real mother and father had ceased to matter long ago.

He exchanged an emotional grin with Steven, his best man and closest mate. What a long way the two of them had come.

And then, there she was . . . walking slowly up the aisle on Tom's fatherly arm. She looked like some kind of perfect vision he'd conjured up in his dreams. His heart did somersaults inside him as she glided towards him gracefully, her eyes fused with his in a look of total love.

This was it, he decided. This was what life was about – what he wanted his life to be about for always. This little girl in the ivory dress who turned his heart and mind upside down.

He was suddenly overwhelmingly glad he'd been through the tough times. Glad about Melissa and the hateful Emily Green, glad The Remedial Class had dumped him, and overwhelmingly grateful to Roo for running out of their wedding. All the events he'd seen as setbacks had actually been lucky breaks – because they'd led him to Summer Bay, to here and now, to exchanging vows with a girl he loved like nobody he'd ever met.

She reached his side and gazed up at him. His heart swelled with such love it hurt. He said a silent prayer of thanks for everything that had gone before, and he took the hand of the girl who would share all his tomorrows.

glossary

The following are Australian terms which you may find used in this book.

Arvo	Abbreviation for afternoon, this afternoon
Heist	Old-fashioned word for robbery
Daggy/Dag	Not trendy, not with it, insulting
Spruiker	Showman, speaks in public
Sucko	To come into favour, ingratiate
Rack off	To get lost, go away
Perving	Voyeur, amorous, stare, checking someone out
Spunk	Good looking, turn on, hot stuff
Crack onto	Make a pass at, chat someone up
Derro	Derelict, drunk, hobo

Really up herself	Snob, too good for other people, full of herself
Chuck sickies	To take days of work/school as sick
Raging	Party, to have fun
Dobber	Someone who tells tales (see dob)
Dork	Idiot, fool
Lamingtons	Slices of sponge cake rolled in chocolate and coconut
Cark	To drop dead
Carny	Abbreviated word for carnival people
Ute	Utility, a car/truck with unroofed carrying section
Pashing	Kissing
Tinnies	Tins/cans of beer only
Dob	To inform against, tell on
Cove	Man